Rose Fire

A Novel by Peter Huyck

‡

Cover Photography Copyright © Anne Markle
Book editing, design and production by Mary H. Mulka

Independently published.
ISBN: 9781081171544

Disclaimer: This is a work of fiction. All names, characters, businesses, places, events, locales and incidents are either the product of the author's imagination or are used fictitiously. Any resemblance to actual persons, establishments, locations or events is coincidental, and on rare occasion incidental, with the exception of the history of the Marian rosary presented herein. This history is as accurate as the author could humanly make it.

Acknowledgements

I am deeply indebted to my editor, as well as to the interlibrary loan office and the reference department at the University of Iowa Libraries, all of which were invaluable resources during the writing of this novel. I am likewise indebted to Anne Winston-Allen, author of *Stories of the Rose*, who encouraged and enlightened me. As I write by hand, I am therefore also indebted to my friend and typist Michael Conroy and his patience in digitizing my endless drafts.

—P.H.

For Cheryl Ann

Chapter I

"May I join you?" he asked.

He sat down before I could reply. I didn't know who he was.

"It is snowing," he observed.

There was over four feet of snow. The airport was closed and the road was impassable. Yes, it was snowing.

We were in the dining room for the noon meal: vegetable soup, homemade bread, and thick slices of yellow cheese. Well, I did sort of know who he was; there were just two of us stranded at the abbey.

On my way here from Chicago, I had driven into a late winter blizzard; my car went off the road and landed in a snowbank. I was rescued by a young farmer with oversized tires on his pickup and a logging chain in back; I got the impression that he was just going around helping poor fools like me.

In fact, I was the last car through before the sheriff closed the road. I had come to gather my thoughts: my employer had eliminated my position, my doctor was talking nonsense, now what, etc., etc.—pressing matters, clearly. When I arrived at the abbey, the guestmaster had said that the snow was deeper, even, than the blizzard of 1886. He said there was a notch on the barn to mark that event. This he considered so remarkable that we must go see it. He pulled on some galoshes, and we headed off through the snow before I had even seen my room.

There was a path, reduced to one v-shaped walking lane, up a low rise, then through some pine trees, then sloping down gently to the meadow that hosted the barn. In the pines, the branches were weighted down to the ground with snow; many had snapped. The old monk kept leading, so I kept following. It was so quiet.

When we reached the barn, he brushed aside some snow with his mitten and proudly showed me the previous record high, three or four inches below the current level. Then, framed by a missing window in the barn, we saw a dead pigeon splayed on some straw. Together, we scrutinized this.

"Someone will die before the new moon," the old monk said matter-of-factly, nodding to no one in particular even though I was standing right there, up to my nose in snow. Strange augury. Was it going to be me? The old monk shrugged; he could obviously not care less if it was going to be him.

We headed back to the abbey, which looked like a fortress high on the hill in the blowing snow. Crows had congregated, taking shelter in the bell tower, calling to each other. It seemed to me a good place to stop for a moment and listen to the snow, but my sturdy and begaloshed guide strode on, and so I followed. Soon I was signing the guest register and hanging up my black suits in my small cell.

‡

Of course, one runs into all kinds in the guest house of a monastery. What draws them there? Around the stranger's eyes a little laughter danced, setting him apart, perhaps, from the desperation in the eyes of the usual nuts.

"I am an alcoholic," he declared. "I quit drinking more than thirty years ago." This by way of introduction.

I knew these sober alcoholics well: cheerful, voluble, forthright, confident. Naive, overbearing, overly familiar, quick to make confidences one just does not want to make. But I didn't particularly want to eat alone. At any rate, he would no doubt be interesting. Pluswhich, it looked like I might be dying soon anyway.

He began, as they often seem to do in my company. Something to do with the Roman collar, I suppose. "I lived alone with my son. Do you know that old camp song *The Foggy, Foggy Dew*?"

> *Now I am a bachelor. I live with my son,*
> *we work at the weaver's trade.*
> *And the only, only thing I ever did that was wrong,*
> *was to court a fair young maid.*

He actually sang this, accompanied by an air guitar around an imaginary campfire.

"It doesn't matter," he went on. "The point is, I was living with my son, sober a couple of years, and I was trying to learn to meditate in order to stabilize my mind."

Outside, it continued to snow.

"Yoga got a little strange. I liked standing on my head, but when the chakras started opening and the kundalini began to rise, I really had no framework in which to understand it. I liked Zen, especially in its purest form: 'We don't believe in anything. We just sit!' But it left me feeling disconnected from my life."

He went on for a while in this vein, then lunch was over, and he excused himself. He walked with a slight limp. I went back to my room and took a nap. This seemed like a

3

reasonable response to the events of the day.

We met again in the dining room for supper. This time I joined him at his table. I'm not sure why.

"You won't believe this," he began.

I supposed he had seen the Blessed Virgin. People who have seen the Blessed Virgin are as common in monastery guest houses as sober alcoholics.

"There was a woman who lived up the street. She used to come and make love to me, then take our laundry home. One day she showed me her rosary. The minute I laid eyes on it, I had to have one of my own."

I looked out the window: still snowing. I looked back at my new friend.

"Prayer beads date back to the early Jain sect. The trade route from Rome to India went up the Nile to the second cataract, then across the desert to the Red Sea — Jain sailors had passed through Egypt for centuries. Have you read the desert fathers?"

I had, but he didn't give me a chance to jump in.

"How unlike Christ! The fierce asceticism, the insistence upon a guru — like wind blowing from the East! Here Christians began to count their prayers. The first one we know of was Paul, near Thebes, in about 350 AD. Right on the road from India to Rome."

He spoke urgently, like it was important I get all this.

"I'm sure you've read Palladius."

I had. *The Lausiac History* is one of our most important sources for the early centuries.

"'There is in Egypt a mountain called Pherme,'" he quoted. "'On this mountain live about five hundred monks, ascetics all. Among them was a certain Paul who led this sort of life: he engaged in no work or business. Now his asceticism amounted to continual prayer. For he knew three hundred prayers by heart, and he would collect that many pebbles, hold them in his lap, and at each prayer cast out a pebble.'"

Just what was it he supposed that I would not believe, I wondered? That his obliging neighbor did his laundry? That the Romans went up the Nile to avoid Afghanistan? That he could quote Palladius? I ran my index finger around the inside of my Roman collar.

He continued, "During the Dark Ages, ascetics from Egypt moved to the islands off Ireland, carrying the custom with them. The Irish brought it to the continent in the 10th century. People counting their prayers on beads. Different prayers, different numbers of prayers, but always on beads."

He waved his arms around a lot. But there was something likeable about him. And at least he had not seen *you-know-who*, or if he had, was keeping it to himself. My friend looked at his watch as if he were contemplating whether there was time before Compline for what he had to say next. There must not have been.

‡

I bundled up and headed outside, only to discover that the front door of the place was now drifted shut. So, I unbundled and walked around the deserted guesthouse instead. The kitchen in the basement was closed; our meals appeared mysteriously from the monks' refectory inside the cloister and our dirty dishes just as mysteriously disappeared afterward.

The monastery was so isolated that the monks seemed to be singing the Divine Office to God alone. The magnificent edifice, built of hand-hewn stone, was surrounded by desolate corn fields. I peered out a narrow window into the inner courtyard, where the drifting snow and the neo-Gothic architecture together formed wild, unfamiliar patterns. The fountain in the middle was a buried shapeless lump. There was a reading room for guests on the second floor, and there I picked up some letters of St. Francis de Sales.

Behind an unmarked door, I discovered a small chapel that must have fallen out of favor. Dust covered everything. I sat down for a while; this was silence within silence. Those who know silence know that it is kind of noisy: beams creaking, snowflakes crashing against glass, squeaky hearts beating, the muffled calls of crows from a bell tower high overhead outside.

At mealtime, I was again regaled with the wild escapades and theories of my newfound friend. It seemed our meals were to be a series of lectures. He watched me sharply, occasionally touching my arm, to make certain I was following what he was saying. And if he saw in my eyes that I might have gotten it wrong, he would erase what he said with an imaginary chalkboard eraser in the air and try again. Was he going to try to borrow money?

‡

After breakfast one morning, he stood up and began to pace back and forth in the slender aisle between our table and the next. By now, there were just a few flakes of snow in the air, but the roads were still drifted shut.

"As one looks back on the broad sweep of the history of the rosary, two figures stand out," he declared. "First, Domenicus Prutenus, an obscure Carthusian monk at St. Albans, Trier, who first added a life of Christ sequence of meditations to the beads around 1415 AD, and second, an unknown woodcut artist who added pictures to the prayer in 1483 AD, at Ulm."

I blinked. My friend erased the air a bit and started over, "All over Europe, since the custom came from Ireland, people were counting their prayers. There were guilds in Paris and London of prayer bead makers. Then enters Domenicus. A drunken school teacher, he was passionate about women and dice. He moved from town to town, involved in endless scrapes. Twice he tried monastic life, only to fail."

He continued to pace, arms flailing.

"Finally, he entered a Carthusian monastery. This time it stuck. It was there, in about 1415 AD, that he first penned fifty meditations to be reflected on as one prayed the beads. This form of prayer spread throughout Europe—more than a thousand copies of Domenicus's meditation were produced by the scriptorium at Trier. In England, it was known as *The Golden Rosary*."

He stopped pacing and sat down. "Those pamphlets, by the way, were the origin of the name 'rosary.' In retelling an old legend about the origin of the beads, the monks in the scriptorium at Trier translated 'rosenkranz,' middle High German for a garland of roses, into Latin as 'rosarium,' a neologism which didn't mean a garland of roses in Latin at all, but rather a rose garden. But ever since, the beads have had this double connotation of rose garden, where lovers met, as well as rose wreath, which lovers wore. 'Rosarium' in Latin became 'rosarie' and eventually 'rosary' in English."

He stood abruptly, then turned to face me.

"The pictures appear in 1483 AD," he said. "At Ulm."

I must have blinked again, because he elaborated: "The pictures of the fifteen mysteries of the rosary. That's when the practice crystallized in the West—when the pictures of the fifteen mysteries appeared. Domenicus's fifty meditations became fifteen, each attached to ten Hail Marys."

This, if true, was news to me.

"There were four Gutenberg printing presses in Ulm," he explained, holding up four fingers and speaking more slowly. I got the impression he might have thought I was a little thick. "*Unser Lieben Frauen Psalter* was first published by Conrad Dinckmut. It consists mostly of one Alanus de Rupe's reflections on the rosary practice, along with a collection of fabulous tales he concocted to promote it."

"The pictures appear at an arbitrary place in the text," he continued, both hands at chest level, as if he were holding an imaginary basketball. "And the blocks were not cut by the same hand as the frontispiece. The pictures and their accompanying text clearly began life as a pamphlet. The printer must have had the blocks lying around, so he just stuck them into a book on a related topic—a common enough practice in the 15th century."

My friend now began to talk in a slightly more solemn voice, hands down and shaking his head slightly. "The artist has never been identified, and I was never able to find anything else by the same hand. The artist, I found, definitely did not contribute to any of the many books published at Ulm, most of which are preserved... but must have instead worked on ephemera, the countless calendars, posters, playing cards, holy cards, horoscopes, and pornography that were printed there."

I think he was trying to shock me. Anyway, his verve was certainly restored. "Cheap playing cards from Ulm flooded the world! They were illegal in Florence, where they were said to threaten their 'artistic tradition.'"

He sat down again and leaned in. "What would people

think if they knew the beads were of Jain origin, the mysteries first conceived by an alcoholic and first illustrated by a pornographer?" He didn't wait for my response. "To me that makes the story more interesting. And more holy."

I noted that his alleged playing card artist was now a confirmed pornographer, but I let the point pass.

Now, he summed up gloriously, looking heavenward with outstretched arms: "The pictures are still alive! They fairly jump off the page when you see them in that old book. They look like they have been beamed in from outer space. They spread all over Europe, copied by many hands. It is *still going on.*"

That afternoon I tried the front door again, and I was able, with difficulty, to pry it open and trudge a path to my car parked out front. It was buried in snow. Looking around, I could see nothing but snow-covered hills. How did I end up here?

‡

The conversation resumed at dinner. My friend dove right in: "The rosary is apparently a good way to come down from a bad acid trip."

I knew by now not to bother questioning, because answers were forthcoming. "There was a 16th century painter, Matthias Grünewald," he supplied. "Matthias did an altar piece in 1515 AD at a hospital in Isenheim that was treating St. Anthony's fire, which is ergot poisoning — essentially, an overdose of LSD from eating moldy rye bread. The series of paintings corresponds to the mysteries of the rosary. It took a long time for someone to figure it out, because they aren't exactly the same fifteen mysteries we know today."

He stood up and started to pace, then stopped short. "The hospital was treating bad acid trips with rosary beads. From the artwork, it is clear that Matthias, too, was suffering from St. Anthony's fire. Moving from image to image, before the retable, reciting the beads, patients clung to their sanity."

My friend began pacing again, fingering imaginary beads and looking at imaginary paintings. He paused. I didn't think he was crazy, but he was certainly *convinced.*

He sat down abruptly and folded his fingers as if to say, now, onto more serious matters. He continued in hushed tones, "I think the pamphlet with the rosary woodcuts that was included in the book at Ulm in 1483 was probably first sold as a prophylactic against the plague. 1483 was a plague year in Germany. Hucksters were selling everything. The idea would have been, recite these prayers on your beads, gaze upon these pictures, and you'll be spared from the plague."

‡

Over breakfast the next day, we talked of inconsequential things. Mostly the snow, which we had already sort of talked to death. Then he began: "One hundred and fifty Hail Marys, one for each psalm in the psalter, and fifteen Our Fathers—those fifteen beads were originally larger and just there to help keep track of the counting. The prayer was added later."

He pulled a jasper rosary out of his pocket, which lit up in a beam of morning sunlight that had glanced through the window off the snow outside.

"So, the Marian rosary has 165 beads—too long. Everyone uses the one-third version of 55 beads and goes around three times. But why does your rosary have 59 beads?" he asked, then waited expectantly.

I pulled mine out of my pocket and looked; he was right, mine had 59.

"Herbert Thurston figured it out," he announced.

Thurston I knew: a Jesuit and towering intellectual figure of the early 20th century. I got the lecture anyway.

"According to Fr. Thurston, the four-bead pendant originated in 16th century England, where three popular prayers were all said on the same strand of beads: The Crown of Thorns with thirty-three Our Fathers, the Bridgettine rosary with seven Our Fathers and sixty-three Hail Marys, and the Marian rosary with fifty Hail Marys and five Our Fathers. The pendant was used for the Crown of Thorns and the Bridgettine rosary, but was not used for the Marian rosary. When the other two fell out of fashion, the people who made the prayer beads eliminated eleven beads from the circle but left the four-bead pendant on, where it now has no purpose. When I took the pendant off my rosary, I felt like I held a real rosary in my hand for the first time. And, indeed, I did."

He sighed. "I pray the rosary every day. To me it is like a spiritual gyroscope—as I go careening through life, caroming from curb to curb, I have this daily practice which lends me some stability. I am drawn—every day—to that spinning wheel. My hand finds my beads and I begin, 'Hail Mary'... it is like a path to follow," he sighed again and looked down, then continued on softly. "There is a hole inside of us—you can't fill it. I can tell you that no matter how much you drink, you can't fill it. But with the beads, the hole vanishes."

Exhausted and slightly out of breath, he continued to gesture about nothing for a while. His look begged me to understand. Then he headed for his room, skipping

Compline. I don't think of myself as a superstitious person, but I did sneak a peek at a calendar in the kitchen; the new moon was the day after tomorrow.

‡

The front-loading plows got through that night, throwing great arches of snow into the frozen fields.

The next day, my friend didn't come to the dining room for breakfast or lunch. He arrived at supper with a manilla envelope. He didn't have much to say. We discussed the condition of the roads. Finally, he pushed the envelope toward me. His eyes met mine, but they were focused on a point further away. I realized that despite our time together, we really knew nothing about each other at all.

"Would you be willing to look at this?" he finally asked.

"Sure," I nodded solemnly, accepting it with both hands. I have long learned that it is usually best to at least give the impression of taking a manilla envelope seriously.

That night, he wasn't at Matins.

The next morning, he wasn't at Lauds.

He wasn't at Mass.

He wasn't at breakfast.

They found him dead in his room.

A phone call was made, and a hearse arrived along with the county coroner. A heart attack in the night, perhaps? An aneurism? The monks carried on unperturbed.

I tucked the envelope into my briefcase. The roads were open, so I dug my car out with a grain scoop and proceeded south.

Chapter II

I took the old river road. In places, it was reduced to one lane by the snow. I was in no hurry, so I took a side trip to some Indian mounds high on a bluff overlooking the Mississippi River. The snow removal in the park was actually better than on the main roads. The trails to the overview were even clear.

I looked over the islands billowing white with snow on the brown river. No one was around. The Jesuits teach that if the hound of heaven is chasing you, you should turn around and see what it wants. They taught something similar in the 101st Airborne, although they phrased it somewhat differently. I called out over the cliff to the river hundreds of feet below.

"What do you want of me?" Silence. So I drove on.

It is a curious breed that lives along the river: sort of low-life mystics. Over breakfast in a café attached to a gas station, I read in a local newspaper the obituary of a man who had spent his entire life fishing for catfish; he chewed tobacco—Peachy® brand—and had kept several black-and-tan coonhounds in succession over the years, all of which had preceded him in death and all of which the obituary actually listed by name. I weighed his life on the scales of the universe against my life, spent teaching paleography to graduate fellows. He seemed to have a slight edge. He was *kind* and *loyal* and *steadfast*; kind to his dogs, loyal to his brand of chewing tobacco, and steadfast in his quest for catfish, surely. No mention was made in the text, for example, of walleye or crappies. As for me?

I drove absently. There wasn't much traffic. People didn't have their cars shoveled out yet, I supposed. I stopped at another cafe for lunch and ordered the special: meat loaf. Through the wide front window, the glare of the sun on the snow forced me to wear my sunglasses indoors.

Later, as I crossed the border into Missouri, I saw a curious business along the road. It looked like a shack and had a long sign on the roof which advertised, "Bait. Liquor. Fireworks. Hot Dogs. Cigarettes." I envisioned how one might spend a lazy day along the river after provisioning there.

Eventually, I had to abandon the old road; I couldn't find it anymore. Fast food franchises began popping up, then acres of condos. It has never been clear to me what, exactly, constituted a condo, but that does not seem to have slowed their development in the slightest. Then, I was forced by virtue of no other southbound option onto the interstate and went flying along I knew not to where.

Well, to St. Louis.

‡

When I finally arrived, they had no record that I would be coming. But after a few hurried phone calls behind a half-closed office door, the staff rushed to make me welcome: "Ahh, yes, of course! Fr. Carl! Let's make you at home!" And so on.

I suppose here is as good a place as any to introduce myself. My name is Carl, and I am a Jesuit priest. The Cardinal Archbishop of Chicago, possibly under orders from on high, had strongly suggested to the administration at the university where I was teaching that this would be an appropriate time to eliminate my chair. Certain findings of mine in certain ancient texts did not quite, it seems, square with Church teachings. I had not been reassigned, so I guessed I was retired. When I asked my provincial, he said that he guessed that I was retired, too. And as such, now, I have found myself here, at the Gethsemane Home: A Community for Jesuit Brothers.

‡

The Gethsemane residents were divided into cliques — I saw that the moment I entered the dining room. I counted seven cliques in all, but there may have been eight: the Traditionalists, the Reactionaries, the Anti-war People, the Liberation Theologists, the Followers of Anthony de Mello (a Jesuit writer from Sri Lanka whose work was condemned by the Pope), the Opus Dei, and the Pentecostals. There also seemed to be a small group of Atheists. They all smelled bad, the odor of dying Jesuits differing not at all from the odor of the rest of the dying around the globe. Which clique would adopt me?

At my first meal, I was joined by the busybodies. It was they who would later hand me off to the appropriate clique unless, of course, I had busybody tendencies myself, in which case I would become one of their own. The ninth clique, I suppose.

There were four busybodies, and they didn't beat around the bush. Over broiled cod, they extracted my age, then, noting I was a little young for Gethsemane Home, began digging into my health. I didn't let them get very far there. Had I opposed the war in Vietnam? (No. Actually, I was in the Army.) Had I worked in the missions? (No. Actually, I was a professor.) What did I think of Fr. de Mello? (I love him, but there was no way I was going to tell them that.) Dessert was institutional cheesecake topped with blueberry pie filling; the busybodies used it to cover their final attack: What the hell was I doing here? I told them I did not know. Lunch over, my social status was left undetermined.

I had an appointment in the office at 10:00 AM the next morning. Was everything OK? Was there anything they could do to make me comfortable? And so on. I was assigned to the hospitality committee, which sponsored happy hour, held once a week on Tuesday night, and the activities committee, which sponsored, among other events, Biblical Trivia Night.

"We all have jobs here!" I was told.

At 10:15 AM, I was deposited in the dayroom to "Relax for a while and mingle!" Everyone sat around and stared into space or watched cable news. There was a nice aquarium in the corner which was supposed to keep those with dementia calm; according to an orange sticker affixed to the glass, it was maintained by a service that maintained fish in nursing homes and dental offices all over St. Louis. They also did apiaries, but we didn't have any birds. Birds were a little more expensive.

On my second day at Gethsemane, I stared into space for a while, then I watched cable news for a while, then I wandered over to watch the fish. Before I was ordained, I used to work as a waiter at the Succulent Pig, a barbeque joint in the West Village near the White Horse Tavern. It was razed and replaced by high-end condos a lifetime ago.

And so it went.

Days I prayed the rosary alone in the chapel. I had

never believed the pious baloney that surrounded it, how Mary appeared to St. Dominic on a dark and stormy night, all this supposedly happening 200 years before the meditations actually made their appearance. Jesuit seminarians are not encouraged to believe in such pious baloney, and I have never had much use for baloney anyway, pious or otherwise.

The food, of course, was terrible. It made me miss the leftover World War II K-rations we used to get in 'Nam. Those came with two pieces of gum, four cigarettes, and four squares of toilet paper. One evening, there was a little buzz in the dining room; there was going to be a panel discussion: "Whither the Order?" I thought I'd skip that.

Instead, I went into the dayroom after dinner. Several old priests were kibitzing a chess game. I sat down behind one of the players. He had an obvious move: K-KB7 MATE. However, he did not move. Two kibitzers left and one new kibitzer joined us; still the player did not move. Finally, I realized that he was asleep.

The next day after breakfast I wandered over to the TV to check the crawl along the bottom of the business news channel. IBM was up ▲0.17. My dear mother left me several hundred shares of IBM, which she bought on the advice of an uncle years ago. I never bothered to mention it to anyone, but I was financially independent.

I thought about starting a conversation with one of the aides who was straightening up some magazines. However, I had noticed that they made notes at the nursing station after conversing with the residents, so I picked up a magazine instead: *Midwest Living*. There was an article about attracting Baltimore Orioles to your backyard. There was also an article about cooking German pot roast, outside, in a Dutch oven. And an advertisement for extra wide shoes, available in widths of E, EE, EEE, and EEEE.

I had decided to return the manilla envelop, so that afternoon I called the guest master at the abbey. He went on and on (and on) about losing the organic certification for their herd, because the cattle ate some hay on which pesticides may have been used while they were stranded in the barns by the snow. At any rate, the monks could not prove that pesticides had *not* been used on that hay. He remembered me and the dead pigeon, but he had no recollection of another guest.

‡

I was watching the fish in the dayroom again. How many days had passed? How many weeks? What were the fish *doing*? Domenicus quits whoring around, sobers up, and joins a monastery. A struggling press operator in Ulm gets an idea for a scam to ward off the plague, and one of the part-timers does a few woodcuts. Next thing you know, I'm stuck in a snowstorm with some crypto-fanatic. An aide tapped me on the shoulder: "You have a phone call in the office, Fr. Carl!"

The connection wasn't very good. Some monsignor on the provincial's staff, I didn't catch his name, apparently following up some other call, had talked to some monsignor on the acting superior general's staff (I gathered *he* had not caught *his* name either) to the effect that I was in Omaha and was everything okay? I replied that everything was okay in Omaha as far as I knew. He seemed also to have actually contacted the acting Superior General himself, who, apparently too polite to hang up, and recalling me only dimly, said that, yes, they were aware of the situation. That was all the monsignor knew. He was also too polite to hang up, so I hung up.

And so it went, until one hot July evening night. Two aides were going to take several of us to a Cardinals game in the van. But the weather looked so threatening, we didn't go. As it turns out, they didn't play; the rain began to come down in sheets at about 7:00 PM. Left with nothing to do, I asked at the office if I could get into my storage locker. Reluctantly, they agreed. I took out the envelope and returned with it to my room.

Inside: a neatly typed script for what appeared to be a one-act play. Why couldn't he have just asked for money?

There was a flash, then a deafening clap of thunder, then the funny *bzzrrrt* of a transformer blowing out. Looking out my window, all of St. Louis that I could see was dark. The home's backup generator started up and an emergency light overhead blinked on. By this dim light, I began to read.

ROSE FIRE

SETTING:

The setting is the interior of a long, narrow, stone church lined on both sides by the stalls of CHOIR MONKS. Outside the windows, it is pitch black. At the far end of the church is the altar, a massive block of granite. The near end of the church has a tier of low benches separated from the monks by an iron railing. Intended for those observing the monks, this is where the audience sits for the play. The organ is on the right, between the railing and the choir stalls. Across from the organ on the left, in space normally empty, is a raised circular stage made of rough wood. This stage is framed for the audience by a giant rosary which hangs improbably from the rafters.

CAST:

The cast consists of six repertoire actors, with two cameo appearances. The actors are in street clothes, specifically jeans, and are in plain sight when not on stage, hanging out in the front part of the monastic section of the church. Actors dress and undress in full view of the audience. Off-duty actors double as stage hands.

COSTUMES & PROPS:

Costumes are minimal, symbolic, and changed quickly. For example, GOD is identified only by a slightly comical turban covered with loosely sewn on penny-sized blue sequins. All props and scenery are similarly minimal and symbolic. Props and costumes alike are to be found lying on wooden benches and from there utilized for the duration.

22

STAGING:

The main dramatic action is on the stage and consists of a series of meditations on the mysteries of the rosary.

During the chanting of each psalm, a threefold story unfolds on stage:

I.   The Old Testament Prefigures the New
II.   The Gospel Account of Jesus and Mary
III.   A Modern Parable of Redemption

These are brief vignettes which rapidly segue into each other, actors playing multiple roles with quick costume changes in each of the three. The first vignette is always an episode from the Old Testament, which is a foreshadowing of the events in the second vignette, which will always be one of the mysteries of the rosary. The third vignette brings these mystical insights into the present, with an account of a modern-day alcoholic, JAY, and his mother EMMA (EM).

All of the action happens on a high stage, under a bright light, surrounded by a giant rosary suspended from the rafters, in front of a darkened monastic choir that is chanting the divine office in the middle of the night.

In attendance, THE ABBOT wears a microphone over his ear and a transmitter on his belt, which he has inadvertently left on, so we can hear clearly his asides to THE PRIOR sitting next to him.

Please note additional Divine Office staging notes in text. All psalmody is from Rosary Psalms.

OVERTURE

The church is dark. A spotlight comes on and finds the cast setting up a tavern in the offstage area: a plank on two sawhorses and outsized flagons. Present are DOMENICUS PRUTENUS (wearing a tight fitting, high-collared jacket with buttons down the front and open at the throat), PEASANTS in crumpled hats, and a young BARMAID holding a rag.

DOMENICUS is playing dice with the PEASANTS, drinking with abandon, and giving the BARMAID the eye. One of the PEASANTS shows DOMENICUS a faded woodcut. They laugh.

PEASANT

(Drunkenly.)

Domenicus, you should have become a monk!

Laughter all around.

DOMENICUS

(Drunkenly.)

I've been kicked out twice.

More uproarious laughter.

DOMENICUS embraces the obliging BARMAID.

The ORGANIST dons a rakish cap and begins to move around the church, playing the tin whistle. He also circulates through the audience.

The spotlight goes out.

When the spotlight comes back on, it finds DOMENICUS alone onstage.

VOICEOVER
Domenicus Prutenus, a schoolteacher in 15th century Germany, addicted to drink and to dice, and powerless over the charms of women, has been run out of town after town.

(The voiceover is a woman's voice.)

DOMENICUS
(Addressing the audience.)

I had been walking through the countryside most of the day, running away again. Toward evening I noticed the ruins of a low wall.

He finds a cardboard piece of broken down wall.

DOMENICUS
Out of curiosity I went over and discovered what had once been a small enclosed garden. Near the center was a pool of clear water fed by a spring. Near the spring, a wild rose was in bloom. I lay down to rest. I must have fallen asleep. When I awoke, I sensed immediately that there was someone in the garden with me.

A WOMAN appears in street clothes (a cotton top and jeans); a simple strand of jasper beads graces her neck. She is singing softly an ancient tune, accompanied by the tin whistle.

WOMAN
I have been waiting for you.

VOICEOVER
Soon thereafter, Domenicus entered a Carthusian

25

monastery. There he composed the first life-of-Christ meditations for the Western prayer beads, which gave birth to the modern rosary.

MATINS

Onstage, DOMENICUS, in the cowl of a Carthusian monk, is kneeling and deep in prayer.

Everything is dark except for the small light over the ORGANIST's music, and the sanctuary lamp, a single candle hanging from the rafters over the altar, at the far end of the church. The bell tolls. We hear the CHOIR MONKS shuffling into their stalls unseen. Then the shuffling stops. Silence. This is matins, the office of the night. A single, old, untrained, cracking voice sings out a capella.

OLD CRACKLING VOICE
Versicle (℣) *O God, come to my assistance.*

CHOIR MONKS
Roaring back.

Responsory (℟) *O Lord, make haste to help me.*

The lights come up to "dim" (so the CHOIR MONKS can see to read).

The cast is just getting it together. The actors are clearing their throats and arranging props in the order they will be needed. For example, two are bringing in the futon. Excitement is building. The actors are curious about the sacred space they now inhabit, but they are not at all intimidated by it, and walk around as if they own the place.

As the actors are occupied, the monks begin chanting Psalm 94. *The chant, which is antiphonal, the* CHOIR MONKS *on one side answering those on the other, begins.*

CHOIR MONKS

Let us come before his presence with thanksgiving;

And with psalms let us sing our joy to him.

The Lord will not cast off his people;

In his hands are all the ends of the earth.

For his is the sea, and he made it;

And his hands formed the dry land.

Let us weep before the Lord who made us.

Exit DOMENICUS.

First Nocturne

Annunciation

EVE has disrobed in full view of the audience and has climbed up onto the stage naked. The CHOIR MONKS *chant. (They can always be assumed to be chanting.)*

CHOIR MONKS

Antiphon *Kiss me, make me drunk with your kisses!*

Your sweet loving is better than wine.

—The Song of Songs

ABBOT

(With mic left on.)

What the hell translation is that?*

*The Song of Songs: A New Translation with an Introduction and Commentary. Trans. Ariel and Chana Bloch. Berkley, University of California Press, 1995.

Listen O daughter, give ear to my words:

Forget your own people and your father's house.

So will the king desire your beauty;

He is your Lord, pay homage to him.

I.

> ADAM, fully clothed, now climbs onto the stage.
> ADAM and EVE move cautiously toward an
> embrace. GOD, offstage, puts on the sequined
> turban.

GOD

(Aside, mugging.)

Who told you that you were naked?

(With dismissive gesture.)

Oh, be fruitful, multiply.

> *Exit ADAM, EVE. They leave hurriedly, as if expelled
> by some force.*

II.

> *EVE now quickly dresses offstage. She returns to
> the stage wearing a light blue scarf which will
> (always) identify her as MARY. GABRIEL climbs up
> after her carrying the wing of a hawk.*

GABRIEL

Hail, full of grace, the Lord is with you. You will conceive
and bear a son.

MARY

How can this be?

GABRIEL

Nothing will be impossible for God.

III.

> *The futon is dragged onstage. An actor holds up a printed photo of the full moon, nailed to a piece of lath, behind the stage. Enter EMMA (EM—the same actress as EVE and MARY) with a sheet that she throws on the futon and proceeds to get tangled up in.*

> *EM is having a bad night. She is sweating and moaning in her half sleep. Suddenly she awakens and sits bolt upright. She seems to remember something that happened, or part of a dream she was having.*

> *Exit EM.*

Visitation

CHOIR MONKS

Ant. *Daughters of Jerusalem, swear to me*
that you will not awaken love until it is ripe.
—Song 3.5

Day pours out the word to day,
And night to night imparts knowledge;
Not a word or a discourse whose voice is not heard.

I.

> *Enter AMOS, dressed as a prophet with a staff. His words identify him.*

AMOS

I was no prophet, nor have I belonged to a company of

prophets; I was a shepherd and a dresser of sycamores.

Exit AMOS.

II.

Enter MARY, ELIZABETH.

ELIZABETH

Blessed are you among women, and blessed is the fruit of your womb. Blessed are you who believed that what was spoken to you by the Lord would be fulfilled.

III.

EM is having a diet soda while her friends are having their third martinis, in outsized, colorful martini glasses at the Golden Calf, a tavern assembled on stage from a plank and two sawhorses. A single neon beer sign proclaims, "The Golden Calf."

EM

I am pregnant.

FRIEND

Who's the father?

EM
(Long pause, looking into space.)

I don't remember.

FRIEND
(Gasping.)

What are you going to do?

EM

I'm going to have the baby.

Silence. Everyone knows how impossibly difficult this is will be.

Nativity

CHOIR MONKS

Ant. *There, beneath the apricot tree,*
your mother conceived you,
there you were born.
In that very place, I awakened you.
—Song 8:5

You are my son.
It is I who have begotten you this day.
It was you who created my being,
knit me together in my mother's womb.

I.

A doll is lying on the stage floor in a reed basket. Behind the basket, one of the actors is rocking some cardboard water back and forth, to look like a river. Enter PHAROAH'S DAUGHTER and two ATTENDANTS in characteristic headgear.

PHARAOH'S DAUGHTER

It is one of the little Hebrews!

ATTENDANT
(Rushing gleefully toward the baby.)

Let me drown it!

PHARAOH'S DAUGHTER
(A terrified scream.)

No!

> *She rushes to the child and picks it up. She embraces the child and dances around joyously.*

A baby! A baby! A baby!

II.

> *MARY, rocking a simple cradle. She is humming a mother's lullaby. There is a brilliant flash of an odd color of light that illuminates everything for a moment: the stage, the choir, offstage, the audience.*

> *A LONE FIGURE appears, as if lost, disoriented by the brilliant flash of light. Who is he? We are never told.*

LONE FIGURE

Where is the newborn?

MARY

Here.

> *The LONE FIGURE comes over and studies the child.*

LONE FIGURE
(A non sequitur.)

No one has ever seen God.

> *Offstage, GOD mugs "Hey!" MARY and the LONE FIGURE continue to study the child.*

LONE FIGURE

Make your dwelling among us.

III.

> *Enter EM. Enter NURSE, with an oversized Red
> Cross lapel pin. She is passing out babies for their
> mothers to nurse. She is carrying three. She checks
> the little bracelets on the babies' wrists (there is a
> little low comedy here as she almost drops one), and
> the bracelet on EM's wrist and finally presents her
> with a baby.*

> *A young INTERN bounds in, in a white jacket.*

INTERN

How are we doing here?

EM

We are doing just fine.

> *(Giving a little ironic twist to "we.")*

INTERN

Do you have a place to stay?

CHOIR MONKS

(℣) *It is impossible to understand the prayer life of humankind
without considering what lies behind the telling of beads.*

(℟) *It is a key to the deepest mysteries of the human heart.*
—C. H. Patton

> *The CHOIR MONKS are seated for the lessons. The
> actors, too, sit down, on the floor or on the benches
> where the props are. A figure appears at the lectern
> who is neither monk nor actor (LECTOR).*

The lessons are read from a very large book which is opened ceremoniously. The lectern is exactly in the middle of the church. The LECTOR wears the same tight-fitting jacket that DOMENICUS wore in the overture.

Lesson i

LECTOR

We first find prayer beads among the Jains around 900 BC. They spread throughout the Hindu sects and later into Buddhism and Islam. They appear in the West in about 350 AD, near the Egyptian town of Thebes. Thebes was on the main road from India to Rome. The Coptics in Egypt still use prayer beads to this day.

From the Egyptian desert, the beads spread to Greece where they are a mainstay of the spirituality of the Orthodox. During the Dark Ages, the beads show up on the islands off Ireland, then move to the Irish mainland, then to the Continent in around 1000 AD. The rosary as we know it came into being in about 1415 AD, when an obscure Carthusian monk at St. Albans, Trier, added meditations on the life of Christ to the beads. The fifteen meditations we use today were cemented in 1483 AD with the publication of some woodcuts in Ulm; the artist who did these has never been identified.

The CHOIR MONKS rise briefly to sing the responsory and versicle each time.

CHOIR MONKS

℟ *More than any other, it was the success of the picture version.*

℣ *That made the rosary attractive to so many.*

—Anne Winston-Allen

34

Lesson ii

LECTOR

A magician gave a genie to a farmer.

"Keep him busy or he will kill you," the magician warned.

The genie cleaned out the barn, painted the house, patched the silo, fenced the pasture, laid some tile, dredged the pond, cleared some brush, mowed along the road, planted hollyhocks by the hog lot. Then the genie began eying the farmer, who rushed back to the magician. What to do?

The magician laughed.

"Give him a ladder. Tell him when he's not working to climb to the top, then climb back down, then climb back up..."

ABBOT

(With mic on.)

Could you run that by me again?

CHOIR MONKS

℟ *Tell me, what do you actually do with a rosary,*

℣ *and what is it all about?*

—Eithne Wilkins

Lesson iii

LECTOR

The practice consists of reciting fifteen times the prayer formula "Our Father..." (Matthew 6:9-13) on the large beads and one hundred and fifty times the formula "Hail Mary..." (based on Luke 1:28, 42) on the small beads. For each set of one Our Father and ten Hail Marys, bring one of the fifteen mysteries to mind.

It is that simple. You will spend the rest of your life exploring its depth.

> *There is a one-person demonstration offstage. A large placard is nailed to a piece of lath. On the placard is the 55-bead rosary described by the LECTOR. The placard is thrust repeatedly into the air, while the actor silently mouths the words, "Fifty-five beads! Fifty-five beads!"*

Second Nocturne

Presentation

CHOIR MONKS

Ant. *Now he has brought me to the house of wine*
and his flag over me is love.
—Song 2:4

I rejoiced when I heard them say:
"Let us go to God's house."
Now our feet are standing within your gates.
O Jerusalem.

I.

> *Enter GOD, looking through a rather long list of items—several pages long. He finds the item he is looking for, then addresses the audience.*

GOD

Consecrate to me every firstborn that opens the womb among the Israelites.

II.

In the temple, indicated by a cardboard pillar and some plastic ivy. Enter MARY and JOSEPH, with doll. Enter SIMEON, carrying a walking stick.

MARY

He is a first-born male.

SIMEON

May I see the child?

MARY gives the doll to SIMEON, taking his cane.

SIMEON

(Obscurely.)

The secret thoughts of many will be laid bare.

The CHOIR MONKS now leave their stalls and gather near the stage. This is their first appearance as the GREEK CHORUS.

GREEK CHORUS

Wait a minute! That wasn't a priest. He just hangs around the temple.

Exit JOSEPH, MARY and SIMEON. But the GREEK CHORUS remains.

III.

The stage is arranged once more as a tavern, the Golden Calf. The ORGANIST plays a little honky-tonk. Everyone is drinking. Enter EM, with doll.

                              EM
Hey, everyone!

                              ALL
Em! Em!

    Cheers all around. Much drinking and
congratulating. EM, no longer pregnant, is making
up for lost time.

                              EM
Beer is good for nursing. His name is Jay.

    An OLD MAN with a cane (the same one SIMEON
carried) puts down his drink and takes the doll. EM
takes his cane.

                           OLD MAN
If there is ever anything I can do, I live right across the hall.

                              EM
That is very kind of you.

                        GREEK CHORUS
    (Alarmed.)

Who is she talking to?

    The GREEK CHORUS monks walk back to their choir
stalls and once more are CHOIR MONKS.

                     Finding in the Temple

                         CHOIR MONKS
Ant. *I sought him everywhere*
but could not find him.

I called his name
but he did not answer.
—Song 5:6

I am wearied with all my crying,
my throat is parched.
My eyes are wasted away
from looking for my God.

I.

> *Enter MOSES with a shepherd's crook. We see a cardboard bush with a spiral-illusion whirligig (apparently from a used car lot) fastened to it. An actor re-spins the whirligig every time it stops. This is the burning bush which is not consumed.*

MOSES

I must go across and see this strange sight.

GOD
(Offstage in sequined hat, mugging.)

Moses! Moses!

MOSES

Here I am.

GOD

Take off your sandals.

> *MOSES removes his sandals. The actor gives the whirligig a final spin.*
>
> *Exit MOSES, carrying sandals.*

II.

Enter RABBI 1 and RABBI 2 in characteristic headgear, carrying tomes.

Enter 12-year-old JESUS, who is identified by a very subtle and understated halo: just a circlet of yellow ribbon caught in his hair. JESUS approaches RABBI 1 and RABBI 2, listens attentively, and seems genuinely puzzled.

RABBI 1
(With exaggerated pedantry.)

If anyone swears by the temple, it has no force.

RABBI 2
(With even more exaggerated pedantry.)

But anyone who swears by the gold in the temple is bound.

Enter MARY. She rushes up, takes JESUS by the ear, and yanks him out of the temple.

JESUS
(Genuinely puzzled.)

Why were you looking for me?

III.

Back at the Golden Calf. Everyone is drinking, including the 12-year-old JAY. People are giving JAY advice.

DRINKER 1
Get all you can while you're young, son...

DRINKER 2

Look out for #1....

DRINKER 3

Do unto others before they do unto you...

DRINKER 4

You only go around once in life...

NEIGHBOR LADY

Did you hear? The old man across the hall has died.

> *EM is devastated. She grabs JAY by the ear and yanks him out of the tavern.*

JAY

Why are we leaving so early?

> *Exit.*

Agony in the Garden

CHOIR MONKS

Ant. *Perish the day on which I was born
and the night that told of a boy conceived.*
—Job 3:3

*In my anguish I called to the lord;
I cried to my God for help.
Fear is all around me,
as they plot to gather against me,
as they plan to take my life.
You are my father, my God,
the rock who saves me.
You are my father, my God,*

the rock who saves me.
You are my father, my God,
the rock who saves me.

I.

>*Enter JOB with a piece of broken pottery. He sits down.*
>
>*Enter FATE. She pours a bag of ashes over JOB's head. JOB begins to scratch himself with the pot shard. JOB, covered in ashes, pot shard in his left hand, is losing it.*

JOB

Lying in bed I wonder, "When will it be day?" No sooner up than, "When will evening come?" And crazy thoughts obsess me until twilight falls.

>*GOD now joins JOB; they pace back and forth, deep in conversation.*

JOB

What are you doing?

GOD

Where were you when I laid the earth's foundations, to the joyful conceit of the morning stars?

JOB

Am I innocent? I am no longer sure.

GOD

>*(Pleading.)*

Have you visited the place where the snow is stored?

42

JOB

Tell me what your case is against me.

GOD

Do you really want to put me in the wrong and yourself in the right?

JOB now gets it; GOD, for some reason, cannot answer him.

JOB

I have spoken once, I shall not speak again. I have spoken twice, I have nothing more to say.

II.

JOB remains onstage. He takes the yellow ribbon out of his pocket and drags it loosely in a circlet in his hair, becoming JESUS. In agony, he kneels to pray.

JESUS

Let this cup pass me by.

A WOMAN approaches with a cup. JESUS drains it.

Let this cup pass me by. But if I must drink it...

The WOMAN approaches again with a cup. Again, JESUS drains it.

Let this cup pass me by. But if I must drink it.... Thy will be done.

The WOMAN approaches yet again with a cup. JESUS just manages to choke it down.

This is most jarring. The last time we saw JESUS he

43

was 12, and his mother was overjoyed to find him. Now he's a grown man of 33 and about to die— pleading for his life. This is intentional and is, in fact, the main action.

III.

JESUS takes the yellow ribbon out of his hair and puts it in his pocket, becoming JAY. Someone passes him half a bottle of whiskey and a rumpled black plastic bag with a few empty cans in it. A parallel shift. We last saw JAY at 12 years old, when he was dragged from the tavern. Now he is a young adult and full-blown alcoholic.

JAY
(Screaming drunkenly, lurching from one side of the stage to the other.)

Why me? Why me? Why me?

On this question, the universe is silent.

Scourging at the Pillar

CHOIR MONKS
Ant. *They beat me, they bruised me,*
they tore the shawl from my shoulders.
—Song 5:7

Take away your scourge from me.
I am crushed by the blows of your hand.
You punish man's sins and correct him;
like a moth you devour all he treasures.
Mortal man is no more than a breath;
O lord, hear my prayer.

I.

Enter JOB, with his pot shard and still covered with ashes, and COMFORTERS 1 and 2 (one a woman).

COMFORTER 1

Job, I speak from experience: those who sow disaster, reap just that.

COMFORTER 2

What knowledge do you have that we do not?

JOB

My foot has always walked in his steps.

JOB lunges at them with his pot shard.

Exit COMFORTERS 1 and 2.

At this point, the GREEK CHORUS rushes forward, fuming with rage against JOB for thinking that he is right and GOD is wrong.

GREEK CHORUS

Can you recall anyone guiltless that perished?

JOB

All perish.

GREEK CHORUS

God is calling you to account for your sins.

JOB

A close reading would suggest...

GREEK CHORUS
(*Enraged; they are having none of it.*)

God is clothed in fearful splendor; he is safe beyond our reach.

JOB has been shouted down but not bested. The GREEK CHORUS monks, however, return to their choir stalls satisfied that right has triumphed.

ABBOT
Little pipsqueak.

II.

JOB takes the yellow ribbon out of his pocket and drapes it loosely in a circlet in his hair. He is now JESUS, who has had a long night dealing with officialdom.

Enter a YOUNG MAN (cameo), dressed only in the sheet from the first mystery. A MAN is chasing him. The MAN grabs the sheet, but the YOUNG MAN slips away naked. (Offstage, he dresses.)

Enter EXECUTIONER with a whip. The EXECUTIONER is full of rage—the rage of the whole human race stranded on this rock—which he takes out on JESUS, striking the stage floor around him repeatedly. An unsettling and noisy scene.

Exit.

III.

Offstage, JAY, trembling, is buying a bottle of cheap wine, with money that he has clearly panhandled (some pennies, a crumpled dollar).

LIQUOR STORE CLERK
Ever think of giving this shit up?

JAY
What the fuck?! You're selling me this shit! And you're telling me I should give it up?

Enter JAY (who still has some of JOB's ashes on him), COUNSELOR 1 (formerly LIQUOR STORE CLERK), and COUNSELOR 2 (formerly FATE, a woman).

The scene is set with three folding chairs and a small table, and some official-looking forms which they bring with them. JAY has found himself in treatment.

COUNSELOR 1
(*Aside.*)

Does he have insurance?

COUNSELOR 2, looking through the papers, gives a slight negative nod.

COUNSELOR 1
How do you plan to pay for your treatment, Jay?

JAY
I don't want any fucking treatment.

COUNSELOR 1
Do you remember how you got here?

JAY
Fuck you.

COUNSELOR 2

It will be to your advantage to cooperate, Jay.

Exit.

CHOIR MONKS

℣ *Highly sensual, inviting continual handling,*

℟ *they were sometimes an ascetic's only material possession.*

—*History of Beads*

All are seated for the lessons.

Lesson iv

LECTOR

How the rosary came to be: In bygone days, a young man went every day to visit a statue of Mary in the ruins of an old stone church. Along the way, he would weave a small garland out of whatever he could find (wild roses in the springtime). He placed the garland on her head, which brought him great joy.

Now it came to pass that our young man felt called to the religious life and entered a distant abbey. But he so missed his daily visits to the statue in the forest, that he decided to leave the cloister and return home. His plans came to the attention of an old monk who suggested he try saying each day the angelic salutation fifty times. This he tried and his joy returned. Years passed.

One day, while riding to a nearby monastery, he stopped and dismounted in a clearing. He took out his beads and knelt to pray: "The Lord is with you. Blessed are you among women." Brigands spotted him there and resolved to steal his horse. As they advanced, they saw a beautiful woman standing before him. She was plucking roses from his mouth and binding them on a hoop. The astonished thieves rushed upon the kneeling monk and demanded to know who the beautiful woman was.

"Woman?" He had seen no woman.

Realizing whom they had seen, the robbers fell to the ground.

CHOIR MONKS

℟   *We live as though we were in Mary's rose garden,*

℣   *All of us who occupy ourselves with the roses.*

—Domenicus Prutenus

> *BRIGANDS with swords rush upon a kneeling MONK with a strand of 50 beads. "Stand and deliver!" (The organist emphasizes this.) A BEAUTIFUL WOMAN is plucking a rose from his mouth. Over her arm, a hoop with more roses bound on it. The Rozenkranz is placed on the kneeling MONK's head.*

Lesson v

LECTOR

One might object that repetition leads to an exteriorization of prayer. That may happen, of course; but then one has made a mistake. It doesn't necessarily happen, for repetition can have a real meaning. Is it not an element of all life? What else is the beating of the heart but repetition? What is breathing but repetition? What objections can one raise against these repetitions and so many others?

They are the order in which growth progresses, the inner kernel develops, and the form is revealed. If it is so everywhere, why should it not also be so in devotion?

—Romano Guardini

CHOIR MONKS

℟ *The words of these prayers are recurrent. They create an open, moving space transfused by energy in which the act of prayer takes place.*

℣ *As soon as the person praying utters the words, he has built for himself a home by his speech.*

—Guardini

Lesson vi

LECTOR

The monotone of the rosary recitation is like the steady beat of a drum, while it also has the rhythmic variation, within tight limits, of those circular Celtic tunes played on the bagpipes out on the hills: a tight pattern of inevitability, of recurrent rise and fall, insistently dancing and marching, and always wide open to the sky. It is this inevitability, this organic drone, that releases the mind into detachment.

—Eithne Wilkins

CHOIR MONKS

℟ *Mary, the mysterious loom of salvation*

℣ *on which the garment of the unity of the two natures was woven in ineffable-wise.*

—Proclus of Constantinople

A MONK has been noisily inflating bagpipes during the reading of the lesson. When it is complete, he plays a brief air such as Wilkins describes, with its tight pattern of inevitability and recurrent rise and fall. Acoustically, the bagpipes tear the church apart.

3rd Nocturne

Crowning with Thorns

CHOIR MONKS

Ant. *For love and for pleasure, his sweetheart had made him a chaplet of roses,
which suited him very well.*
—The Romance of the Rose

Their hearts tight shut, their mouths speak proudly.
They advance against me, and now they surround me.
Now that I am in trouble, they gather, they gather and mock me.
They take me by surprise and strike me and tear me to pieces.
They provoke me with mockery on mockery and gnash their teeth.

I.

  Enter JOB, tearing his hair.

JOB

They smite me on the cheek insultingly; they are all enlisted
against me.

  (Covering his ears.)

As their provocation mounts, my eyes grow dim.

  (Pounding his skull.)

My days are passed away, my plans are at an end, the
cherished purposes of my heart.

II.

  *Enter JESUS wearing a crown of thorns over his
  halo. Enter RABBLE; they are very drunk. They
  notice JESUS standing there.*

RABBLE

Hail! King of the Jews!

(Laughter.) They keep falling down and making comical salutes.

DRUNK 1

Hail! Jew of the kings!

DRUNK 2

Jew! King of the hail!

DRUNK 3

Hail, hail! The king Jew!

DRUNK 4

Hep! Hep! Jing of the Poohs!

They all find this hilarious.

RABBLE

Jing of the Poohs!

Jing of the Poohs!

Exit.

III.

Enter JAY and five AA MEMBERS (three of them women), all wearing Harley-Davidson bandanas and all carrying folding chairs. Someone sets down a pyramid-in-circle emblem, and we are at an AA meeting. (The emblem looks like this: △.)

JAY

My name is Jay. My P.O. says I have to attend three of these classes a week.

AA MEMBERS
(*Overly cheerful.*)

Hi, Jay!

JAY

I got a third DUI. The DMV took my license for six years. My ex is still using. DHS has the kids.

AA MEMBERS

Easy does it, Jay.

First things first, Jay.

Do you have a sponsor, Jay?

Keep coming back, Jay.

Remember Jay: "Think, think, think!"

JAY
(*Aside.*)

I wish I could stop thinking.

> *Everyone now holds hands in a circle and chants with exaggerated enthusiasm.*

LEADER
(*Sing-song.*)

Who is large and in charge?

AA MEMBERS
(*Sing-song.*)

Our Father, etc., mumble mumble *(sic)*.

Keep coming back!

It works!

But you have to work it!

Every day!

(*With emphasis.*)

HEY!

Carrying the Cross

There is an old legend that a beautiful woman, VERONICA, stepped out of the crowd as JESUS passed by carrying the cross, and wiped the sweat from his brow. We're getting to this.

CHOIR MONKS

Ant. *You have ravished my heart,*
my sister, my bride,
ravished me with one glance of your eyes,
one link of your necklace.
—Song 4:9

They go out, they go out, full of tears, carrying seed for the sowing.
I am a pilgrim on the earth; show me your commands.
I will run the way of your commands; you give freedom to my heart.
Guide me in the path of your commands; for there is my delight.
Your commands have been my delight; these I have loved.

I.

Enter 12-year-old DAVID twirling a sling, acting bravely to cover up his fear. Enter WOMAN wearing the jasper beads. Their eyes meet.

54

David.

She hands him a polished stone for his sling. DAVID heads out, shouting bravely.

DAVID

I come against you in the name of the Lord of the Hosts, the God of the armies of Israel.

II.

Enter JESUS, VERONICA (wearing the jasper beads) and ADMIRING WOMEN. JESUS is dragging an imaginary cross. VERONICA approaches him and tenderly wipes his face.

JESUS

Do not weep for me; weep instead for yourselves and for your children.

VERONICA wipes his face, gives him a drink, and crushes him to her breast. Subtext: There is hope for the future of the human race.

III.

Enter JAY and three female AA members (AA WOMEN). All are wearing Harley-Davidson bandanas and carrying folding chairs. One is wearing the jasper beads. One carries the ⬠ sign, which she sets on the floor.

JAY has got this AA thing down pat now. The WOMEN listen to him with rapt attention and open admiration.

It doesn't matter if you believe. Pretending to believe what you don't believe won't get you sober.

AA WOMEN

(Sigh.)

JAY

You will have direct experience of God. Then you will believe.

AA WOMEN

(Sigh.)

JAY

Get your program off the page.

AA WOMEN

(Sigh.)

Exit.

Crucifixion

CHOIR MONKS

Ant. *Love is as fierce as death.*

Even its sparks are a raging fire,

a devouring flame.

—Song 8:6

My God, my God, why have you forsaken me?

~

They tear holes in my hands and my feet

and lay me in the dust of death.

I can count every one of my bones.

These people stare at me and gloat;

they divide my clothing among them.

They cast lots for my robe.

~

Into your hands I commend my spirit.

I.

> *Enter ABRAHAM and ISAAC (cameo). ISAAC is very*
> *trusting. ABRAHAM raises a dagger to slay ISAAC.*
> *In rushes GOD; he is definitely not mugging.*

GOD

Abraham! Abraham!

> *He is trying desperately to prevent ABRAHAM from*
> *making a stupid, tragic mistake.*

ABRAHAM
(Coming out of a fog.)

I thought you wanted me to kill him.

GOD

I didn't want you to kill him. I wanted you to release him, so he could find his own way.

> *ISAAC steps forward, and he and GOD speak*
> *animatedly together, out of ABRAHAM's hearing.*

All exit.

II.

> *All is dark. There is a blood-curdling scream. As we*
> *listen closely, we realize it is two blood-curdling*
> *screams, a man's and a woman's, intermingled.*
> *Suddenly, the spotlight comes on. JESUS, dressed*

only in a white smock with the yellow ribbon circlet in his hair, his arms outstretched as if crucified, is screaming. MARY stands nearby, also dressed in a white smock, with the blue scarf, also screaming. They scream together in an operatic duo, for quite some time, moving together around the stage as if in a somnambulistic dance.

Enter DEATH in an expressionless white mask. She joins the dance. The screaming gradually stops. JESUS and MARY are holding hands. DEATH gently removes MARY's hand, then takes JESUS' hand herself and leads him offstage.

III.

JAY, ill, is lying on the futon. A NURSE attends him, with her back to the audience. Jay's AA FRIENDS, in Harley-Davidson bandanas, come to visit the hospital.

AA FRIEND

(In response to an unheard question.)

Hep C. He was on the waiting list for a liver.

They seem to know the NURSE from the program.

...Brenda?

...Brenda!

When the NURSE turns around, she is wearing the big red cross but also the white mask of DEATH. Now EM (as the organ crescendos), offstage, restarts the screaming. She runs to the far end of the church and throws herself down in front of the altar (a clear violation of the actors' assigned space), where she remains, sobbing. Two MONKS leave their stalls and approach her gently. They help her up and lead her back to the offstage area.

CHOIR MONKS

℣ *In gardens, beauty is a byproduct.*

℟ *The main business is sex and death.*

—Sam Llewelyn

ABBOT

Huh?

All are seated.

Lesson vii

LECTOR

Troubadours and monks used the same language. The religious mysticism of the Middle Ages is cloudy with eroticism, and the love poetry has a mystical, floating quality.

—Wilkins

CHOIR MONKS

℟ *Breath upon my garden, let its spices stream out.*

℣ *Let my lover come into his garden and taste its delicious fruit.*

—Songs 4:16

Lesson viii

LECTOR

The spirit of prayer finds expression in words that die to deliver up their meaning. With every utterance silence grows in height and depth and the soul, rising on the wings of words, finds itself within Silence, wherein, for a few brief moments, the soul enjoys a kind of sleep—in a meditation without thought, a concentration without effort, a colloquy

without words; it is caught up, as it were, in the immutability of Him who Is.
—Fr. James, O.F.M. CAP

CHOIR MONKS

℟ *If God draws you forcibly while saying the rosary, make yourself passive in his hands.*

℣ *Let God work and pray in you. This will be enough for the day.*
—St. Montfort

An offstage actor puts on a nun's wimple, which she finds among the props. This is unaccountable, as the wimple never appears onstage. Regardless, she is now THE NUN. She moves forward and makes an announcement in a mock nun's voice.

NUN
There will be desecration of the rosary at 11:00 AM Saturday in front of Planned Parenthood.

Lesson ix

LECTOR
The monotony of these repetitions clothes the poor old woman with physical peace and recollection; and her soul, already directed on high, almost mechanically, by the habitual gesture of drawing out the rosary, immediately opens out with increasing serenity on unlimited perspectives, felt rather than analyzed, which converge on God. She allows her soul to rise freely into a true contemplation, well worn and obscure, uncomplicated, unsystematized, alternating with a return of attention to the words she is muttering.
—J. Maréchal

ABBOT
Deep.

CHOIR MONKS

℟ *Building up in the long run, on the mechanical basis they afford*

℣ *A higher, purified, personal prayer.*

—Maréchal

ACTOR

(Offstage banter.)

Have you ever watched those nuns say the rosary on TV when you're stoned?

CHOIR MONKS

Collect

Hence it is clear that the rosary cannot be dismissed as a popular piety, but rather is an advanced tool for mystical union with God.

—Edward L. Shirley

Thus Matins is concluded.

The rain had let up a little. Outside, I watched the neighborhoods coming back on, one by one. Then my lights came on. The dim little emergency bulb blinked out.

My friend had based his revision of the office of the feast of the rosary on the breviary promulgated in 1960. That was during the reign of John XXIII, but before Vatican II. The breviary was revised again, shortly thereafter, at the direction of the Council; the 1975 edition basically obliterates the feast.

The next day, I put the manuscript in my newly acquired safe deposit box at the bank, along with my will and medical power of attorney. The day after, I got it back out.

I resolved to show it to the director of the home, and so arranged a meeting with him before lunch that day. After glancing at it, he suggested that I might like to write up a little piece on it for our newsletter, *Gethsemane Home Happenings*. Of course, it is very important at the home to never give any indication that you might not be in your right mind, or off you go to memory care. So I nodded noncommittally, as did the director.

I spent the afternoon furious, at the director of the home, at the acting Superior General, at the Cardinal Archbishop of Chicago, at the man who died and left this curious manuscript with me. I angrily watched the fish in the day room. Then it came to me.

As we used to say in the 101st Airborne: "What the hell?"

Rumor had it that the abbot began drinking wine after Compline, so I waited until exactly 8:45 PM before I called — he should be feeling expansive by then, but not yet garrulous.

"This is Fr. Carl," I began.

"Of course, Fr. Carl!" he shouted. Bingo!

I revealed to him my proposal.

Chapter III

The abbot *adored* the idea of producing the play at the abbey. He remembered the author, too, but could not place his name. It seemed my friend had actually consulted him on a small matter once. The abbot was intrigued by the revision of the old office, which he loved and missed. Could I send him a copy of the script? He himself would play The Abbot, of course, he averred, quick to share he was in fact quite the thespian in his seminary days. Then he dropped a bomb: he was friends with the chairwoman of the drama department at the College of Martin Luther, a private liberal arts college in the nearby town. Perhaps she would like to get involved? He gave me her number, made me promise to get right back to him, thanked me for having thought of him, and had another glass of wine, which I know because I could hear him pouring it. A rather generous pour, it sounded.

The next day I wandered around the day room. At Gethsemane, the old war protesters thought the Anthony de Mello crowd was a bunch of pansies. The reactionaries thought that the war protesters had destroyed the Order. The de Mello crowd itself was seeking the Holy Grail of de Melloism: not needing any human approval. I hoped they would succeed, because the Liberation Theology bunch certainly was never going to approve of them. Cable news was interviewing moderate Muslims who were trying to allay everyone's fears about the rising horde. The fish seemed agitated; was it going to rain again?

Since I didn't know the drinking habits of the chairwoman of the drama department at Martin Luther, I didn't know exactly when to call. Something told me, though, that wine was probably involved somehow in her friendship with the abbot. So I chose 5:30 PM the next day.

When I called, she answered after one ring. She had obviously talked to the abbot already and was expecting my call.

"Before you ask," she said excitedly, "the answer is yes." Not only was the answer yes, but she already had a plan. Or, rather, they had a plan: I could detect some of the abbot's touches. She would offer a course in the spring: *Medieval Religious Drama (with Practicum)*; I would teach it as an adjunct instructor (no benefits). I could stay at the monastery for the semester, which was only a fifteen-minute drive from campus.

"I was thinking four credit hours," she said. "To account for the practicum, of course. Don't you agree?"

"Sounds about right," I agreed. "What kind of involvement might we expect?"

She was waiting for that question and promptly laid down her aces. "I think probably *all* of our best drama students will want to enroll."

"I don't know you," I told her, "but you have made me a curiously happy man." My ticket out of the old folk's home was now officially stamped.

I promised the chairwoman I'd send her the script. She thought we should have dinner to discuss some details before class started.

"Do you plan to do just Matins, or are you going to finish Lauds?" she asked, curtailing my goodbyes. How could she have possibly known that there was no Lauds?

"To be determined!" I answered cheerfully and hung up.

From the front office, I both made and mailed off photocopies of the script to the abbot and the chairwoman — in manilla envelopes, the same way I had received it. Now all of the sudden I was floating above my peers: I had something to *do*.

‡

As for the chairwoman's question, I sat in front of the giant fish tank in the dayroom, pouring over the script. I had already come to the conclusion that it must end with Lauds: Matins, Intermission, Lauds. The rosary, after all, depends for its efficacy on the resurrection, the descent of the Holy Spirit, and the coronation of Mary. The power is in the present reality of these mysteries. Otherwise, they are just worry beads. The problem with this conclusion was its clear implication: I was going to have to write Lauds myself.

I purchased a blank book at a stationary store in a strip mall near the Gethsemane Home. I also bought a nice new pen. When I got back to my room, I lay the book open on my desk. I uncapped my new pen. I then went and watched the fish for a while. Then I went and watched cable news for a while. Is there ever *nothing* happening? Then I returned to my desk, only to be confronted by the still-blank page. Domenicus Prutenus's alcoholism was the key to the whole piece, it seemed, and I knew absolutely nothing about it.

In this regard, my having landed a coveted position on the hospitality committee served me well. At the next weekly happy hour, I worked the snack table: aerosol cheese product (spread on store brand snack crackers) and lil' smokies (sausages served in "BBQ sauce"), which were to be eaten with the assistance of toothpicks, a box of which was provided.

Happy hour at the old folk's home was a sad affair. I mean, even besides the ersatz barbeque sauce. For one thing it lasted *exactly* one hour. Men arrived promptly at 5:00 PM—some brought guests—and at 6:00 PM everyone immediately decamped. Second, the music. This was provided by such aides who fancied themselves musicians. According to the committee's budget ledger, they got paid for the hour of playing, but they did not get paid for rehearsing, which they had clearly not done much of. Still, happy hour boasted a healthy attendance, and sure enough, from my key snack-table vantage point, I soon spotted a priest who wasn't drinking.

I wandered over and began to talk in a general way about not drinking. It was like a large mouth bass hitting a lure; in no time, he was telling me his whole life story and how he had quit drinking and joined Alcoholics Anonymous. This was "Father Bill."

I told Fr. Bill about the strange circumstances that had led me to seek him out.

"I know the office, I know the scriptures, I know the rosary. But of alcoholism I know nothing," I concluded. "Perhaps you could fill me in?"

I don't think he had any idea what I was talking about, but he did gather that I wanted to know more about AA. He proposed taking me to a meeting, and so, after dinner, we went.

The AA meeting was held in a storefront in the mostly abandoned strip mall where I bought my blank book and pen. Motorcycles were parked out front, as was a crowd of people smoking cigarettes.

We made our way to the door. An occasional attendee

hailed Fr. Bill. Then, the meeting began. After a few brief and somewhat disappointingly as-expected preliminaries, people began talking. A number of them had been in prison. The women were generally battered and damaged, clinging to a slender reed, hoping that they might get themselves back together. All of their lives were being worked out in terms of un-understandable and remote bureaucracies: the courts, the motor vehicle department, the unemployment office, the welfare office, the veterans' administration, treatment centers, halfway houses, parole boards, vocational rehab, the police... it was endless. Yet here the fragile flame of faith flickered. There was laughter. They seemed to care for each other. There was a clear recognition of the enemy: for them, it was alcohol.

A young woman was telling her story: "I had two finals the day after my birthday. So I decided to not go out, but to stay home and study. But a couple of friends came over and wanted to buy me a pizza, so I decided to go with them and have just two beers then come home. So I ate some pizza and drank two beers and then..."

Everyone was laughing before she got to the punchline: "And then I changed my mind."

This fetched the house.

Chapter IV

Things were coming together up north. The course was in the Schedule of Courses, a night was set for dinner with the chairwoman of the drama department at her condo, a date was set for the performance at the monastery, the organist was already inquiring about music and even making suggestions. And I still had not finished the script.

I have published eleven books in my lifetime. I do not recall ever being "at a loss for words." But every time I sat down at my desk, shiny new pen in hand, my beautiful still-blank book would only mock me.

So I watched the fish and cable news. I decided to read some William ("Bill") Wilson, the founder of AA, who wrote *Alcoholics Anonymous*. Wilson was a synthetic thinker, fusing the propositions of an early American psychologist, a Swiss psychoanalyst, a Counter-Reformation bishop, and a 19th century Russian anarchist with 1st century mysticism. A good read, I suppose. But still I couldn't finish Lauds.

Chapter V

The Gethsemane Home ran a sort of rent-a-priest racket for the local diocese. Anyone who was ambulatory and more or less in his right mind was liable at a moment's notice to be called on to say mass somewhere for someone in the greater St. Louis area. Late that fall, I was asked on behalf of a local priest to cover his parish over the weekend so that he could, allegedly, keep vigil with his dying mother. Since this involved both a 5:00 PM Saturday Mass and a 7:00 AM Sunday Mass, I would stay at the rectory Saturday night.

The parish was apparently accustomed to having their regular priest missing, as the deacon was at my shoulder every step of the mass, giving subtle stage directions. I used a canned homily which I keep on hand for just such occasions. (Actually, I have five of these which, I hasten to add, I canned myself.) I can deliver them without much thought, and the congregation, clearly accustomed to lesser preaching, goes away feeling that they have been touched by fire. "Did you hear about that Fr. Carl? He's a Jesuit," and so on, as they file out.

I enjoyed the luxury of staying up with the late-night shows Saturday night, then went contentedly and drowsily to bed. The quiet bedroom was all 19th century: a huge oak dresser, an enormous crucifix, and a narrow, uncomfortable bed.

At about 2:00 AM, I was awakened when the doorbell of the rectory insistently rang. I had a little trouble finding the front door, being in a strange house, but I finally swung it open and found two St. Louis police officers flanking a young man who was obviously quite drunk.

I recognized one of the cops; he had received communion from me at the 5:00 PM Mass. I tried to remember which of my famous homilies I had delivered earlier that might have inspired the officer's compassion.

"We found this guy talking to a parking meter," he said. "Claims he was trying to call a priest."

I could see that they were trying to give the guy a break, as well as save themselves some paperwork, so I said, "You can leave him here with me." This they did; they were off the porch and down the drive before I could shut the door.

My new charge and I adjourned to the parlor. He was dark, rather short, with a thin mustache. I offered to make him some coffee, which he declined. He pulled out a pack of cigarettes, but it was empty.

"Shit," he said.

I pointed out that there was an all-night convenience store two blocks away, and that I would be glad to buy him a pack of cigarettes if he wanted to walk down there with me. It wasn't really safe to walk in this neighborhood at night, but I figured that with him along and me in collar, I would be OK.

As we walked along the street, he was effusive in his gratitude: "Thanks so fucking much, man," and "I really needed to talk to a fucking priest, man." He had a slight accent which I couldn't quite place. I think he was probably in a blackout; he had that strange glazed-over look in his eye — like no one was home.

‡

The convenience store was kind of a rough place, more so this time of night. It looked like just about anything could be bought right in the parking lot. The windows were plastered over with beer signs; the sidewalk was covered with blackened circles of chewing gum. I looked around. No one appeared to be actually chewing any gum.

"Hey, you lookin' for a lady?" a man accosted us. Perhaps he didn't see my Roman collar. Or, perhaps he did. My accomplice took my arm, clearly giving the signal: this guy is with me.

Inside, the cashier was seated behind bullet-proof glass. I had never purchased anything through bullet-proof glass before. I ordered a pack of Chesterfield Kings and a quart of beer. It was pay-in-advance. I slipped my money into a tray and slid it through a narrow slot. The cigarettes came back under the glass, the beer through a curious-looking interlock.

"How about a book of matches?" I asked. The clerk looked at me as if to say, you want me to call the law?

"That's OK. It doesn't matter," said the now tender voice of my charge. Or was I his charge?

"You don't know what you're missing," the pimp taunted across the parking lot as we headed back toward the rectory. I found a certain irony in this remark, but, glancing around, it looked like no one else was picking up on it.

The beer was in a brown paper bag, which my companion had quickly modified to be form-fitting around the bottle. Good. I didn't want to look conspicuous. My charge was now smoking greedily and had opened the beer.

"What smokes are these?" he asked.

"Chesterfield Kings," I said.

He gave the finger to a passing car and shouted, "Chesterfield Kings!"

"Fuck you!" they shouted back.

When we got back to the parlor of the rectory, my charge sank into the couch, while I improvised an ashtray. I also brought a glass for his beer, but apparently he preferred to drink out of the bottle, which was still in the bag; he didn't even touch the glass.

"Father, I have sinned...," he began, then turned suddenly belligerent again.

"Have you ever ridden a long winning streak, when you just *could not lose?*" he demanded. I remained silent. When I left my mother's home for New York City, I thought I was on a winning streak when I got on at the Succulent Pig right away. Looking back, of course, I know I was just a pretty boy and willing to work for next to nothing.

But that's not what he was talking about. He was talking about couldn't lose turning into couldn't win turning into couldn't stop. I think.

"Have you ever had a woman tear you down until you vanished?" He leaned in close with this one, like: what did I know?

I could not answer. I supposed he was talking about sex. I have never had sex, which, seeing as I am a priest, shouldn't be too surprising. But I have had that sense of vanishing. I didn't attempt to explain it to him; I have had it in prayer. One day, kneeling at the altar, I vanished completely. A few moments later, I reappeared. I'm sure that this is what he was talking about. Could this be why men drink and chase women?

Then he waxed sort of philosophical: "There isn't enough beer in all of St. Louis to slake my monstrous thirst," he said with glassy eyes. I thought that this was rather well-put, and I took a closer look at him, thinking that I might have overlooked something. But he was getting incoherent. And then he passed out. I let him sleep on the couch. Of course, there is a great deal of beer in St. Louis.

In the morning, he was gone; just a damp spot on the couch roughly the shape of Madagascar. That was it. Nothing special. But when I got back to the home after Mass, I began to write. I wrote late into the night, and before morning, the script was complete.

LAUDS

Lauds opens in a completely darkened church. During the office, the lights are gradually brought up so that, by the end, every light in the church is blazing.

A conservative element of CHOIR MONKS has caucused during intermission to form the CONSERVATIVE CAUCUS. They come forward. They want to have their say. (All comments are from the Roman Breviary, *1960.)*

CONSERVATIVE CAUCUS
When the wicked heresy of the Albigensians was growing in the district of Toulouse...

CONSERVATIVE MONK 1
St. Dominic, who had just laid the foundations of the Order of Preachers, threw himself whole-heartedly into the task of destroying this heresy.

CONSERVATIVE CAUCUS
He implored with earnest prayers the aid of the Blessed Virgin, whose dignity these errors shamelessly attacked.

CONSERVATIVE MONK 2
As everyone knows, she instructed Dominic to preach the rosary to the people as a unique safeguard against heresy and vice.

CONSERVATIVE CAUCUS
St. Dominic began to promulgate and promote this pious method of praying.

CONSERVATIVE MONK 3
And the fact that he was its founder and originator has been

from time to time stated in papal encyclicals.

One of the CONSERVATIVE CAUCUS monks, a crabby old reactionary, steps forward and raises a finger in the air.

CRABBY MONK
All to the contrary is...

His voice is shaking. His finger is shaking.

Anathema!

He loves the word "anathema." Shaken, he returns to his stall. A female actor wanders over and lovingly musses the old man's hair. Just as it looks like the office can finally get started, some OTHER MONKS move forward and speak. (All comments are from the encyclical Marialis Cultus {Paul II, 1974}.)

OTHER MONKS
The council has denounced certain devotional deviations, such as vain credulity, which substitutes reliance on merely external practices for serious commitment.

OTHER MONK 1
Another deviation is sterile and ephemeral sentimentality, so alien to the spirit of the Gospel.

OTHER MONK 2
Study of the sources will prevail over the exaggerated search for novelties or extraordinary phenomena.

OTHER MONKS
It will ensure that devotion is objective in its historical setting, and for this reason everything that is obviously legendary or false must be eliminated.

With extra emphasis there at the end.

The OTHER MONKS return to their stalls. Now can we get started?

CANTOR

Oh God, come to my assistance.

CHOIR MONKS (ALL)
(Roaring back.)

Oh Lord, make haste to help me.

Resurrection

The archetypes of the mysteries of Lauds are taken from the New Testament.

CHOIR MONKS

Ant. *Look, winter is over,*
the rains are done,
wild flowers spring up in the fields.
Now is the time of the nightingale.
In every meadow you hear
the song of the turtle dove.
—Song 2:11,12

For the poor who are oppressed and
the needy who groan
I myself will arise, says the Lord.
I will grant them the salvation for
which they thirst.

I.

A MAN begins to sow wheat on stage. Then he begins

to sow in the offstage area. One actor imitates a bird grabbing a seed and taking off. Another actor imitates a young plant withering for lack of moisture. The MAN then begins to throw wheat into the choir stalls and into the audience. The result is kind of a mess, like the rice left on church steps after a wedding.

II.

The stage is empty. JESUS shows up sort of disorientated (with halo), and looks around. MARY MAGDALENE appears. She is wearing short shorts, fishnet stockings, stiletto heels, a scoop-necked blouse, and a rosary as a necklace.

ABBOT

Jesus!

At this all the CHOIR MONKS pile out of their choir stalls and rush forward, surrounding the stage to form the GREEK CHORUS. We just got them settled, now here they are again.

GREEK CHORUS

No! *This* is a desecration! A whore with a rosary!

MONK 1

My grandmother brought her rosary *from Ireland.*

MONK 2

My aunt has a rosary that was *blessed by the Pope.*

MONK 3

My rosary has been in the family *for five generations.*

JESUS

(Aside.)

Did anyone ever use it?

GREEK CHORUS

In short, we cannot and do not and will not condone this.

JESUS

Will you continue to sing?

GREEK CHORUS

We have been singing the Divine Office since 600 AD. We will sing.

The GREEK CHORUS monks return to their stalls and, after a little petulant fussing around, resume singing as CHOIR MONKS. So, it seems that the friction within the choir is more serious than we thought.

Back to the story. This scene consists of exactly two words, with a lot of meaning packed into them.

JESUS

Mary.

MARY MAGDALENE

Teacher.

III.

Enter EM and AA MEMBERS. One carries the △ sign; all wear Harley-Davidson bandanas. All are seated. The sign is placed on the floor, announcing that this is an AA meeting.

This AA meeting is JAY's funeral.

AA MEMBERS

(In turn.)

Jay helped a lot of people, Em.

I remember when he reached out to me.

Jay was good AA.

He is at the big meeting in the sky.

I wonder if those beads he carried around really helped.

Helped with what?

(Pause, thinking how to phrase this.)

Nameless fears.

EM

I should think they would be just the ticket for nameless fears.

Our AA meeting is transformed into the Golden Calf. The AA sign is knocked over. The BARTENDER is thrown a bar rag.

BARTENDER

Full of fear and anxiety? Johnny Walker—liquid courage.

Pursuing unachievable goals? Fuel your pursuit with Budweiser.

Angry at the boss? Furious at your ex-wife? Smirnoff. That'll show 'em.

The BARTENDER casts the bar rag aside, someone

sets the ⊕ *back up and sits down. The meeting resumes.*

AA MEMBERS

Let's have a moment of silence for Jay—an alcoholic who no longer suffers.

He never had a sponsor. But, he died sober.

Ascension

CHOIR MONKS

Ant. *Who is that rising like the morning star,*

Clear as the moon,

Bright as the blazing sun,

daunting as the stars in their courses.

—Song 6:10

O gates, lift high your heads;

grow higher, ancient doors.

Let him enter, the king of glory!

I.

A KING appears. Three SERVANTS file in. The KING gives each SERVANT some gold coins. The KING then vaults offstage, and then reappears, climbing up the iron steps. The first SERVANT steps forward.

SERVANT 1

Sir, your ten gold coins have earned ten more.

KING

Well done.

SERVANT 2

Sir, your five gold coins have earned five more.

                            KING
Well done.

                          SERVANT 3
Sir, here is your coin back. I was afraid.

                            KING
You were afraid.

II.

> The actors carry a large papier-mâché rock onto the
> stage with two black footprints on it. Now everyone
> looks up. This tableau occurred in every woodcut of
> the Ascension in the 15th century. So let them stand
> there and look up for a while, until the audience
> maybe gets it.

III.

> Now the stage is cleared. GOD in the blue sequined
> hat and JAY in his Harley-Davidson bandana, are
> pacing back and forth.

                            GOD
It's really easy to become an AA saint; you can swear, chase
women, smoke cigarettes—all you really have to do is stay
sober and help others. Becoming a Catholic saint is *much*
more difficult.

> GOD is rolling His eyes and mugging some self-
> flagellation. He shakes His head.

Descent of the Holy Spirit

> It is told of Bill Wilson, the founder of AA, that when
> a woman thanked him profusely for her sobriety, he
> replied simply, "Pass it on." Everyone should just be
> keeping this in mind.

CHOIR MONKS

Ant. *You are a fountain in the garden, a well of living waters.*
—Song 4:15

He sends out his word to the earth and swiftly runs his command.
The Lord's voice resounding on the waters,
> *the Lord on the immensity of the waters.*
The voice of the Lord, full of power,
The voice of the Lord, full of splendor.
The Lord's voice flashes flames of fire.

I.

> *Jesus and Mary.*

MARY

They have no wine.

JESUS

How does this concern me?

MARY

> *(Indicating to all present.)*

Do whatever he tells you.

II.

> *Everyone is onstage, milling around silently. Suddenly, everyone begins talking at once, rapidly, loudly.*

> *The GREEK CHORUS rushes forward.*

GREEK CHORUS

They have been drinking too much new wine!

ANY ACTOR

We're not drunk. It is only nine in the morning.

GOD

It will come to pass in the last days that I will pour out a portion of my spirit upon all flesh.

III.

We are at an AA meeting. JAY's spirit is alive.

AA MEMBER

We don't care what you believe—AA is not based on belief in God. AA is based on conscious contact with God. If you are not sure whether or not you have had conscious contact with God, you haven't had it. The steps are just words. They point off to concepts. These in turn point off, imperfectly, to the shimmering realities in terms of which you will find the solution.

SOMEBODY

Uh, what?

Assumption of Mary into Heaven

CHOIR MONKS

Ant. *Who is that rising from the desert like a pillar of smoke,*
more fragrant with myrrh and frankincense than all the spices of a merchant!
—Song 3:6

My heart rejoices, my soul is glad
even my body shall rest in safety
You will not leave my soul among the dead,
nor let your beloved know decay.
You will show me the path of life,
the fullness of joy in your presence.

I.

GOD

(*In a mild rage.*)

Go out quickly into the streets and alleys of the town, and bring in the poor, the crippled, the blind, and the lame.

> *Everyone (some in Harley-Davidson headgear) piles onto the stage again: actors, ushers, understudies, the ORGANIST. They begin to "party," even though there is barely room to stand.*

II.

> *There is an ancient legend that the apostles assembled at MARY's deathbed. So, here MARY lies dying. The APOSTLES gather round (anyone who is handy). The same question is on all of their minds. However, no one asks it.*

III.

AA FRIEND 1

We never saw her again.

AA FRIEND 2

She may have gone out.

AA FRIEND 3

Someone thought they saw her at a meeting in Chicago.

> *EM is in a wheelchair, in a nursing home. She has a jasper rosary which she is reciting slowly. A perky ACTIVITIES DIRECTOR comes up and insists she come to the common room and work on a puzzle with the other patients.*

CHOIR MONKS

The condition of human nature is such that it has to be led by things corporeal and sensible to things spiritual.
—Sanctity Through the Rosary

Crowning of Mary as Queen of Heaven

CHOIR MONKS

Ant. *Let us go early to the vineyards to see if the vine has budded, if the blossoms have opened and the pomegranate is in flower. There I will give you my love.*
—Song 7:13

The lot marked out for me is my delight: welcome indeed the heritage that falls to me! The daughter of the king is clothed with splendor, her robes embroidered with pearls set in gold.

I.

> *GOD appears. He is looking around, worried. Offstage, a woman (DAUGHTER) swirls through riotous living in pantomime. She stops.*

DAUGHTER
(Out loud, to herself.)

I shall go to my father and say to him, "Father, I have sinned against heaven and against you. I no longer deserve to be called your daughter. Treat me as if you would treat one of your servants."

> *She climbs the stairs. GOD sees her.*

GOD

Quickly, bring the finest robe and put it on her; put a ring on her finger, and sandals on her feet.

A dour OLDER DAUGHTER climbs up and, hands on her hips, looks disapprovingly on.

II.

GOD crowns MARY with a chaplet of roses.

III.

EVE/MARY/EM is alone onstage, crowned with roses. She looks radiant. Suddenly, she takes off the crown and sails it into the audience, like a frisbee or a bridal bouquet. She heads for the offstage futon and falls down dead. Someone pours some stage blood on her.

Two DETECTIVES appear in wide-brimmed fedoras. They look for clues. One finds a cheap rosary. The CHIEF OF DETECTIVES also now appears. He, too, wears a wide-brimmed fedora.

CHIEF

What have we got here, boys?

DETECTIVE 1

Murder.

CHIEF

Find anything?

DETECTIVE 1

Not much. Drug paraphernalia, condoms.

DETECTIVE 2

There was one thing...

CHIEF

What's that?

DETECTIVE 2

She had a cheap plastic rosary which was broken and repaired in two places, once with a paper clip, and once with dental floss.

He holds up the rosary. There is a long pause as the CHIEF OF DETECTIVES works this out.

CHIEF

(Inspecting the rosary.)

Hmm. You don't usually think of a prostitute using dental floss.

The GREEK CHORUS comes forward for the last time.

GREEK CHORUS

The power of beads is such that there must be hidden within them some meaning common to us all.

—History of Beads

The GREEK CHORUS monks return to their stalls.

Little Chapter

CHOIR MONKS

To whom shall the racked of body and agonized of mind go in the long dark hours of the sleepless night?

—Silent Bedes

Benedictus

CHOIR MONKS

Ant. *We live as though we were in Mary's rose garden, all of us who occupy ourselves with the roses.*

—Domenicus Prutenus

He swore to grant us

That, delivered from the hands of our enemies,

we should serve him without fear

In holiness and justice before him all our days.

The CHOIR MONKS file out. The actors (onstage and off) are left unsure exactly what to do next, and so kind of bow a little and then just wander away to mingle.

Finis.

Chapter VI

Shortly after Thanksgiving, I undertook to clear the way for my absence. The director of the nursing home said that I was technically still under the authority of the provincial of my last assignment. The provincial's vicar at my last assignment, however, would not return my calls. I gathered that no one at Gethsemane had ever wanted to *do* anything before, so the question had never come up. So, I just left.

I packed my car. I took some clothes (five black suits, a pair of slacks and a polo shirt), my golf clubs, Volume IV of the old Breviary, and my rosary, which I had modified early that morning to 55 beads, with a pair of needle-nose pliers that the janitor lent me. By bending a few wires, I was able to remove the four beads that had so offended my friend. I figured, if I was going to do this, I might as well have a 55-bead rosary, too. After modifying it, when I looked down at it in my hands, I had the same odd feeling that he had mentioned: that I was holding a real rosary for the first time.

I had a great sense of freedom heading north on the old river road that I had headed south on last winter. I wondered if I could find the same cafe. I wondered what the special would be. Chicken and noodles? Sirloin tips with rice? *Roast pork with dressing?*

I love the little river towns, the mom-and-pop motels with mom and pop still at the helm. I like catfish. I like the shabby Friday nights, the gut bucket music, the women in tight jeans, the drunks lurching toward their pickup trucks in the tavern parking lots. Here, all was as right with the world as it was ever going to be.

My little sojourn amongst the moribund had taught me one thing: the end is ever nigh. In my mind's eye, I died. I saw a decent funeral. Would my Methodist cousins come? Their children? Certainly not their children, who were probably busy with jobs and families by now, and who barely knew me anyway. Would any of my old colleagues come? Those who had crossed sabers with me over issues that had seemed so important at the time? What of my memorial fund? $25 and $50 checks sent by those too busy to attend the funeral. Would it be enough money to get some birds for the big day room? Probably not. The Superior General, suddenly remembering who I was, would surely send his adjutant. The Bishop, too, would send some monsignor as his representative. Some of the staff from the home would come, as they are required to do, and the residents capable of sitting up independently and taking nourishment... who else? But how many fine suits I had for the mortician to choose from!

I turned my attention resolutely toward the curious path that had opened up before me. As I drove along, I revisited Lauds in my mind. The resurrection, the proof, and the promise. I don't know why, if they had never experienced any of these things, anyone would want to believe in them. Faith just means, if something happens, you don't think it's something else.

I stopped again at the bluff with the Indian mounds. The park was again empty. I walked up to the overlook; very still there. I felt no need to cry out this time, though. No one knew where I was. A priest's is a lonely life. You get used to it. I didn't stay at the overlook long.

‡

I drove along, not thinking of much, occasionally returning to the actual conundrum of my existence these days: how to get some young Lutheran drama student to take her clothes off in church, as scripted, Act 1 Scene 1.

Around a bend in the road, someone had converted an old gas station into a lot full of folk-art whirligigs. I turned right in. The gas station was so old that the driveway was gravel. Rusted-out signs advertised automotive products long since forgotten. There were about fifteen elaborate contraptions on display, made from bicycle wheels and tin-snipped beer cans, all driven by the wind.

I got out of the car and was swept up by the wonder of shifting and turning and spinning. Their profound movements meant nothing at all, served no purpose, summoned no God.

An old man emerged from a nearby trailer and walked over, his boots crunching in the gravel. I half expected him to ask, "Fill 'er up?"

"You make these?" I asked.

"Yup," he nodded.

"Do you sell many?"

"Nope."

He spat. We stood in silence except for the humming and squeaking and chattering that surrounded us, courtesy of the wind in the whirligigs.

"I don't really have any place to put one," I apologized.

"That's what everyone says," he shrugged. "They look OK in front of a trailer off in the woods. Sometimes I attach a flower box — for geraniums," he added, then looked at me defiantly. "You a priest?"

"Yup," I answered. This got him to crack a smile.

"Perhaps you understand," he said, gesturing toward his creations dancing and swirling in the wind. For it is written: The wind blows where it will.

"Chaw?" he asked, pulling a plug of tobacco out of his pocket and offering it to me. I used to chew — back in the 101st. There were times when it wasn't a very good idea to light a cigarette.

I looked at the bluff behind the station. It rose almost straight up. High above, some eagles glided in the updraft. Or they could have been vultures. A crow was calling from a dilapidated barn across the highway. Behind it, the quiet river. A gust of wind suddenly turned all the whirligigs about face. They whirled and jangled and clattered. I looked at the deliciously grubby plug of tobacco. I looked into his blue-gray eyes.

"No thanks," I said. "But thanks."

I crunched back over to my car and the car crunched back onto the old river road.

‡

Since I wasn't expected at the monastery until the next day, I spent the night at the Bide-a-Wee, a mom and pop motel along the river. You could read the history of the river from its facade, so many times had it been under water. I asked "Mom" where I could get something to eat; she said the tavern.

Accordingly, I headed over to the Dew Drop Inn & Eats, a peeling clapboard sort of place set into the bluff a half mile down the road. When I entered, it was empty. I took a booth. Several deer heads were mounted on the wall, among neon signs advertising domestic beers. Two huge jars, one boiled eggs and the other pickled pigs' feet, flanked the bar, along with an oversized canister of beef jerky.

The waitress, a worn and plain-looking woman, maybe in her thirties, maybe not, came out from the kitchen, stood at my tableside, and stared.

"Do you have a menu?" I asked.

She waved at a chalkboard with a hand-scrawled list on it. Tuna and noodles was crossed out; the lunch crowd must have finished those off. Next: liver and onions. I hate liver and onions.

On the wall was a faded cardboard sign which read "Frozen Pizza Burgers."

"I think I'll try the frozen pizza burger," I said.

"Pizza burger!" she shouted.

"Pizza burger!" someone shouted back from the kitchen. Then, rather than returning to the back of the house, she sat down to join me in the booth.

"You a preacher?" she asked.

"No, I am a priest." The distinction was clearly lost on her.

She smiled. I smiled.

"I hate liver and onions, too," she confided.

"Well, it seems we have a lot in common." My irony, however, was also clearly lost on her.

"The guys don't get here until about 7:30," she offered, smoothing her apron.

"The guys?"

"That work on the barges," she replied.

I looked at my watch: 6:10 PM. "Would you care to join me for dinner?"

"Sure," she shrugged.

"Bart!" she hollered. "Hot beef with fries!"

"Hot beef with fries!" the male voice hollered back.

I love hot beef sandwiches. "I didn't know you had hot beef," I said.

She detected my envy. "You can have some of my fries."

I heard the fries hit the grease in the kitchen. Next there was the tell-tale ding of a microwave: my frozen pizza burger was done. Then there was another ding: the little bell that called the waitress to the serving window. She got up and brought our food; she also brought me a carton of 2% milk with a straw and herself an oversized diet cola. And ketchup.

I bravely waded into my burger after removing it from its too-hot cellophane envelope. Surprisingly, it wasn't too bad — possibly because I was so hungry. But I kept stealing glances at her magnificent hot beef sandwich, nearly drowning in its pool of brown gravy. She squirted ketchup over her fries and gamely shared them with me.

We chewed in relative silence.

"Do you want a piece of pie?" she asked.

"Sure."

She got up and brought back two towering slices of raisin cream pie. It is hard to find good raisin cream pie these days. "Raisin pie is Bart's specialty," she explained.

After the pie, she lit a Chesterfield King.

AA has a curious custom: Instead of confessing to a priest, they just confess to another human being. Just so long as that human being is still alive, it counts. I looked at my dinner companion; here, clearly, was a living human being. Maybe I could confess to her. I was sure the barge workers did it all the time, after a few drinks.

"Do you mind if I tell you something?" I asked. She shrugged, indicating that, since I was buying dinner...

I had trouble getting this out. She waited.

"I killed some men. In Vietnam," I finally said, my voice falling flat over our un-bussed dishes.

"War is hell," she replied, not a beat lost on her end. She looked mildly interested.

"Young men. Just boys, really. I have never told anyone."

"They give you preachers a gun?" she asked.

"I took a weapon off a dead body. Our position was being overrun."

"Why you telling me? You ain't drunk."

"I wanted to tell someone, I guess."

She shrugged again. "Anything else?"

"I have never been in love," I said, but I have no idea why I said it.

"You ain't missed much," she replied, exhaling deeply and stabbing out her cigarette.

I began to try to calculate the incalculable: how much to tip. $50 was out of the question, but $100 seemed like a fat gesture—like over-tipping in Las Vegas. I considered $300. It would be way beyond a fat gesture, but then she might think I wanted sex. So what I came up with was $900—surely beyond her thinking I wanted sex, short of $1,000, which would again be fat gesture. I paid at the register, then handed her $900 in $50 bills.

"Thank you for listening," I said.

"Hey," she said, taking the money and shrugging her shoulders yet again. She got it, that I had used her, alright. She glanced around to make sure Bart wasn't watching, then slipped the fifties into the pocket of her apron. Behind the register, on the wall, was a crude pencil drawing of a barge on the river.

"Who did that?" I asked, nodding toward it.

She looked at it kind of proudly. "I did."

"Well, I like it," I said, and I left.

The next morning was beautiful. Are there different kinds of beauty? The grain elevators, the rusty barges, the abandoned rail road sidings I was passing were beautiful; beautiful, too, was river, the islands, and the eagles (or vultures?) above. But different. The whirligigs were beautiful. The waitress at the Dew Drop Inn & Eats was beautiful. They all made me want to smoke. If I went back to smoking, the cigarettes could not possibly kill me as fast as I was already dying. But still, I didn't go back.

‡

As I drove along, I saw an older man on crutches by the side of the road, hitchhiking. He had two artificial legs. Assuming he was a veteran, I stopped the car; we could talk about 'Nam. His sorry belongings were in a plastic bag, which he heaved into the back seat. He leveraged his way into the car with great difficulty. There was silence.

"How did you lose your legs?" I asked a few miles later. I'd had a friend, a nurse, who had lost her legs in a helicopter crash.

"Hobo camp," he supplied. "Ten below zero. I had a blanket, but some sonofabitch stole it. Legs froze. Gangrene. Nothing else to do but amputate, they said."

We rode in silence for another mile.

Then, "They did good work," he allowed charitably, gesturing toward his prosthetics and nodding vaguely northwestward. "University Hospital."

So much for talking about 'Nam, how the helicopter pilots used to ice down beer in the body bags, and so on. We rode in silence for perhaps another ten miles.

"Where are you heading?" I asked. He was evasive.

"How far are you going?" was his answer, another mile later. Clearly, he would be happy enough to go wherever I was going.

"Dubuque."

"You got people there?" he asked.

"I am going to the monastery." It was only then that he noticed that I was a priest.

"You a priest?" he asked.

"Yes. I am a priest." That was it for conversation. He kept muttering to himself, though—it almost sounded like he was praying in tongues.

When I stopped for gas, I asked him if he smoked. "Sure!" he said; all was forgiven. I asked the cashier for a pack of Chesterfield Kings, but they didn't carry them. They have been getting harder and harder to find. I noticed a young man playing video poker, and so I just got a pack of whatever he was smoking. My passenger was glad enough to get them.

"Do you mind?" he asked.

"No," I lied. He lit one. My eager nostrils picked up a whiff of smoke. Decidedly not a Chesterfield. We rode in silence again, but the silence had changed: all of a sudden, the silence was listening.

"Are you from around here?" I asked cautiously. He did not reply.

I have few regrets. I could have visited my poor dear mother more often, I suppose. And I suppose I could have presented my findings a little more tactfully over the years.

My passenger was snoring. Suddenly, I felt a little anxious. The thought occurred to me: suppose God wanted to talk. What disguise would He wear? Wouldn't it make sense for Him to take the form of a hobo with no legs, so that I would pick Him up thinking He was a veteran, so we could talk about 'Nam?

I looked carefully at my passenger; he looked a little like a drawing of God: long gray hair with a beard. I rode with Him, while my hobo friend slept on. This was my chance to get some answers.

I thought about what to ask. I had some questions about the Church. I had some questions about tobacco. On the other hand, I thought I could appreciate some of the difficulties He's had establishing an outpost on this rock hurtling through space.

There is something I want you to do.

I was overwhelmed by an emotion that I had never felt before and could not name; the only way I could express it was "thank you." This I said out loud. My passenger stirred and muttered in his sleep.

I let him out at a hobo camp outside Dubuque, down where the tracks run along the river. Then I drove on to the monastery. The abbot met me at the door. "Fr. Carl! We have been expecting you," he boomed and quite nearly brought me in for an embrace. It was Sunday.

Class didn't start until the second week of February. I had six delicious weeks all to myself, as a "special guest" at the monastery. Christmas was bliss, New Year's Eve was silent—no one here was banging on a pan with a spoon. In January, I went on a silent retreat. No one spoke to me, nor did I speak to anyone, for the entire month.

Chapter VII

On Friday, the first week of February, I drove to campus to see how long it would take me to get there, and then located my classroom, so I wouldn't get lost looking for it on the first day of class. I was assigned to a small theater with a raised stage—rather quaint. The room was painted entirely black with track lighting overhead; assorted staples, pieces of tape and splotches of paint covered the walls. There was a copy of the Schedule of Courses on one of the chairs; I leafed through it. There it was: *16: 337 Medieval Religious Drama (with Practicum), 4 cr., vis. Prof., 211 Theater Arts Bldg. T-TH 3:30-5:20.*

I located the campus bookstore, where I bought a maroon hooded sweatshirt with "The College of Martin Luther" printed across the front in bold white letters. I wear a small, so the lettering was kind of cramped. I also picked up the scripts at the campus copy shop. How fine they looked, stacked alternately and separated by pink sheets of paper.

Monday morning, I found a hand-written note taped to my door at the monastery; I was invited to address the community at Chapter (7:00 PM) to explain what I was doing there. Good question.

At Chapter, deep in the bowels of the monastery, the monks all sat in a circle. I was in the circle with them. The abbot introduced me as "Our guest, Fr. Carl, of the Society of Jesus." This brief introduction skipped over some material: there was no mention of the books I had published on ancient manuscripts and my recent scrap with the Cardinal Archbishop of Chicago. Probably just as well.

I stood and began: "I am in possession of the script for a theatrical work that is meant to be performed in front of a group of monks singing the Divine Office in choir. The abbot has graciously consented to let me use your church for a performance of the work."

This generated only mild curiosity.

"I will need some volunteers to chant," I continued. "The actors will be college students from town. There will be a small temporary stage across from the organ. The stage will be on wheels, so it can be moved out of the way and left in the cloister when not in use."

Still not much in they way of reaction or response, so I described how I came to possess the manuscript originally. Everyone had fresh memories of the snowstorm, and a few remembered seeing the script's author in church. Their story of losing organic certification for the cattle, of being forced to use some hay that could not be certified organic, was told yet again, and the proctor went off on a ten-minute tangental rant about the difficulties of getting someone buried when no one knew exactly who he was.

When the conversation finally returned to our matter at hand, I started to detect some suspicion in the circle. I hoped for eleven monks in the choir, plus the organist and the abbot. My approach was this: ask for volunteers first, and, if none of the suspicious volunteered, why worry about them?

Six younger monks volunteered straight away, showing that they were hip and jumping at the chance to escape the monastic monotony, or perhaps just currying favor with the abbot, who was known to be in my camp. One by one, four older monks then volunteered; it was not clear to me whether they understood what exactly they were volunteering for. None seemed particularly suspicious, though. I was one short.

There was a long pause.

The abbot looked hopefully around the circle. I looked hopefully around the circle. Then one of the older monks seemed to volunteer precisely *because* he was suspicious. Great.

This was Fr. Javier. He walked with a gnarled oak cane. I approached him after chapter.

"Good to have you aboard," I said.

I later learned from the organist that Javier had been in Vietnam during the very early years of the war, whereas I had arrived toward the end. He had been an intelligence officer with an advanced unit and spoke fluent Vietnamese, which he had learned at Yale, courtesy of the U.S. Army.

"I thought someone should keep an ear on you" he replied.

I knew what he meant. He had trained himself over the years in the cloister to listen (that was actually his job in the army, too), and he intended to listen. We stood there, me hoping for a word of reconciliation. He was in no hurry, as monks frequently aren't.

"Cardinal Mahoney is an idiot," he said at last. So, he knew about Chicago.

"Good luck casting Eve," was his parting shot.

Wait a minute. How did he know about that?

‡

Class did not begin until Thursday, but Wednesday was my dinner with the chairwoman of the drama department. I arrived at her condo with a bouquet of three pink roses courtesy of the local supermarket. At precisely the time agreed on (6:00 PM), I rang the bell.

"I am so happy to finally meet you!" she exclaimed as she opened the door. Her blouse was low cut, her gray-streaked black hair in a tight bun. I tried to get by with a sincere handshake, but, with a subtle twisting motion, she turned it skillfully into a full embrace.

Even though it was February and still quite cold outside, she had the grill going on the patio. I noticed two New York strip steaks on the counter between the kitchen and the dining area. The candles gracing the table had been lit a considerable time earlier in the evening, judging from the wide pools of wax congealing at their bases. There was a trench coat draped over the arm of the couch, and before she slipped through the French doors to tend the grill, she likewise slipped into the trench coat, then back out upon her return. She poured two glasses of wine, then plopped herself down on the couch. I lured her to the table by simply sitting down there instead.

"Do you always wear that Roman collar?" she asked, as she arranged my roses in a tall vase.

I usually reply "except in bed" when asked this question, but that didn't seem appropriate here. Instead, I changed the subject.

"The thing we must ask ourselves," I began, "is what do we have here, and why are we doing this?"

She laughed at me. "The thing we must ask ourselves," she countered, "is whether you want ranch dressing on your salad or Italian. And how do you like your steak?"

That stopped me in my tracks. "Medium rare, and I'll try the Italian," I said.

I had raised a finger to make a point, but since there was

no point to be made, my finger just sort of hung out in mid-air.

"Eat your salad," she laughed.

I actually like iceberg lettuce. I has been occasionally suggested to me — constructively, I suppose, and usually by nuns with whom I'm on retreat — that I am kind of a snob. But not about food. At the Succulent Pig we had precisely three sides: baked beans, coleslaw, and potato salad.

The chairwoman slipped her trench coat back on and ducked out to the patio to fetch the steaks from the grill. Then she sat back down across the table from me and leaned forward. I told her a little about myself, playing up getting run out of Chicago. Since she was in theater, I developed the cast of characters and reenacted some of the major scenes from the Inquisition. I told her how I had come by the script, entertaining her with my impersonation of the author. I left out my stint in the 101st Airborne. She seemed to get that I was too young for the nursing home.

She told me a little about herself: studying theater arts out East, trying to make it in New York, finally moving back to the Midwest. Then she paused, having come to the hard part. I shrugged slightly; had I not left out a big part myself?

"I think the abbot would like a bigger part," she said. I just nodded slightly. I hesitated to modify the original script for Matins. Could I add something for him to Lauds?

By now we were about halfway through our steaks.

"Well, who all has signed up?" I asked, as if we had just cast our course into "Catalog Lake" and were sitting back on shore waiting for a bite. What I really wanted to know, of course, was what was the chance of getting one of them to take her clothes off.

I think the chairwoman had decided to let me suffer. She mentioned the need to accommodate a student named

Cassie and her wheelchair, and a difficult student named Marley [?] (her mouth was full), that apparently no one knew how to deal with—so I was on my own—but whose father gave a lot of money to the College of Martin Luther's Century of Excellence fund.

The evening was over. There was a little mischief in her eyes: she clearly knew something that I didn't know.

We closed with another full embrace—there was no other way.

"Goodnight, Carl," she said. "Nice to finally meet you."

"Indeed," I replied.

When I got to the car I found a worn copy of a thin book—just a pamphlet, really—entitled *Improv!* in my coat pocket. When had she put it in there? While I was in the bathroom? During our embrace?

‡

There is a small cemetery in a churchyard across the road from the monastery. I drove in. It was a clear, cold night; the moon was full. Spotting the shallow indention of a recent grave on the lawn, I walked over to read the inscription on its marker: "Unknown. d. March 17, 1998. May God have mercy on his soul." My heart raced. He was here, under the sod.

"Well, here I am," I said.

"I wasn't really doing anything anyway," I added.

Some lovers pulled into the gravel drive in a van, so I yielded the cemetery to them, with its dark and the quiet.

Back in my cell I took out my beads to finish my rosary. I was on the 13th mystery—the descent of the Holy Spirit.

"Hail, full of grace, the Lord is with you. Blessed are you among women, and blessed is is the fruit of your womb." I have always preferred the ancient form of the prayer.

"Hail, full of grace...," again.

My thoughts wandered.

The day of Pentecost. The disciples gathered in the upper room. I thought of myself standing at the podium on the small stage. One of the track lights was focused on me. Fourteen well-scrubbed but faceless students sat before me. The beat-up stadium seating receded into the blackness. There was a noise like a strong driving wind.

Chapter VIII

The next day was the first day of class. That morning, I was downtown picking up a few items when I ran across a strange little storefront. It wasn't clear to me just what exactly it was that the shop sold, but they did have Cat-in-the-Hat hats in the window, in a variety of colors. My dear mother used to read *The Cat in the Hat* to me. So I bought a Cat-in-the-Hat hat with a nice yellow stripe. The store clerk said (and I quote), "Whatever, man."

I arrived at my classroom promptly at 3:30 PM, dressed as usual in an impeccable black suit and Roman collar, and wearing my yellow Cat-in-the-Hat hat. My students were already seated. "Jesus Christ!" someone muttered. That was good, as I had hoped to develop an informal atmosphere.

The fourteen students sat in a semicircle of fourteen desks facing me on the stage of the little theater. The auditorium seats were taken from an old movie theater and still had ancient pieces of gum stuck on the bottom of them. They sloped gently up to the spotlights in back. Shoved in a corner of the stage were a number of props left over from previous productions: a kitchen table (*A Streetcar Named Desire?*), a small wooden bridge (*Our Town?*), a row of paper sunflowers (*Oklahoma!?*), etc. There was a podium and lectern on stage, whether pedagogic aid or old prop (*Mark Twain Tonight!?*), I couldn't say.

"Okay," I said, stepping to the lectern. "In two months we are going to put on a play out at the Trappist monastery just south of here. Some of the monks will also be involved and we will be rehearsing with them later in the semester. You will all get A's." I began passing out the scripts. "Please feel free to interrupt me at any time if you have a question."

A hand went up.

"Yes?"

"Who is going to take off their clothes in church?" was the question.

I wondered how they had gotten their hands on a script already. There was silence. Then there was giggling. I stepped off the podium and looked over my glasses.

"Tryouts will be held Week 4," I said, then returned to the podium.

"The play is about the Divine Office, the rosary, and alcoholic drinking," I said. "This will be covered in Week 2. Week 3 we will begin readings. Today I will tell you a little bit about myself and how I came to have this script. Put your notebooks away."

All the students wore sensible boots; it was February, after all. Puddles were forming on the floor beneath each pair; it had finally snowed. Fourteen backpacks were leaning against their chairs. I began to wonder what was in their backpacks. Granola bars? Tuna salad sandwiches? Cigarettes?

"My name is Carl," I began.

A few students re-crossed their legs. Someone muttered "Hi, Carl!" to a low chorus of snorts in response.

"When I finished college, I headed for New York City, as so many used to do and, I suppose, still do. I was making it 'on the scene' as they say, more or less trading in on my youthful good looks." I could see that they didn't know where I was going with this. Good.

"I ended up waiting tables at a high-end barbecue joint

in the West Village near the famous White Horse Tavern: the Succulent Pig. Here I was known as 'Shorty.' As you can see, I am short." I stepped away from the lectern, stepped off the podium, then removed my Cat-in-the-Hat hat to emphasize this last point.

"You may call me 'Shorty.'"

"Hi, Shorty!" One of the girls, wearing a bulky green wool sweater, tried it out, extending the syllables, "Shorr-teee." This got a little laugh.

"One night, after the barbeque joint closed, the whole staff headed over to a jazz club. The music was strangely unsettling. It was Thelonius Monk."

I paused for their reactions, expecting something like "You mean you have actually heard Thelonius Monk in person!?" However, they seemed never to have heard of him. So I just continued.

"Sitting at the table with my co-workers, I had a startling experience. I was never able to explain it to anyone, or even to myself, really, but the result was that I converted soon thereafter to Catholicism. I took instruction at a little church on the corner in six Sunday night sessions... five, actually, as I recall one Sunday got canceled because of snow. My co-religionists were all basically secular souls preparing to marry one of the beautiful Italian girls who still lived with their mothers in the neighborhood."

I attempted a little improv while telling all this: how we held our trays at the 'Pig, how the crowd swayed at the jazz club, the eagerness of the young men in their anticipation of marrying beautiful Italian girls. I couldn't really tell if this amused my students or not; their expressions hadn't changed much since I took off the hat.

"Soon after that I joined the Jesuit Order," I continued. "My studies took me to Rome, where I was ordained a priest by Pope John XXIII. Then, I was drafted into the army. After I got out, I got a PhD and spent most of my life teaching paleography at various Catholic universities in the United States and Europe."

A young woman in tight fitting jeans and an embroidered natural cotton top, wearing a strand of jasper beads and a magnificent pair of cowboy boots, tentatively raised her hand.

"What is paleography?" she asked.

I spent two years in the 101st Airborne, 18 months of it "in country." Vietnam. The 101st would parachute into a firefight, then the chaplains would accompany the medics, coming in on helicopters. It was very noisy. This unsaid.

"Paleography is the study of old manuscripts," I said. "Today you will be leaving early. Class dismissed."

My students grabbed their backpacks and headed for the door, their boots now dry. But the girl in the cowboy boots hung around. She was a several inches taller than me, perhaps 5'8".

At that moment, the chairwoman entered the room. "Yoohoo! Carl!" she said. I swear: "Yoohoo!"

"Oh, hi, Chloe," she added, pronouncing her name without diaeresis to rhyme with "sloe," as in "sloe gin." It seemed the chairwoman was going to be very proactive. I felt like I had started chasing a gum wrapper in the wind, had totally lost my bearings, and now was chasing something else entirely, with no hope of ever catching it.

The chairwoman offered Chloe a ride back to her dorm, which she accepted.

‡

On Tuesday I arrived again promptly at 3:30 PM, impeccably dressed as usual and wearing my stupid yellow Cat-in-the-Hat hat. The desks were inexplicably gone, and the students were seated instead here and there in the theater seats. I took my position behind the lectern on stage. Two students had already dropped the course after the first session. This hurt my feelings, especially since I had promised everyone A's. But the script only called for six repertory actors. This I had, plus plenty left over.

"Who remembers the big snow last year?" was my opening remark.

Everyone did. Days without power, running out of food, classes canceled for a week. A sister's baby born at home.

"I was journeying from Chicago to St. Louis and got stranded by the snow at the monastery. There is a retirement home for Jesuits in St. Louis, which is where I was headed. There was one other person at the monastery snowed in with me. A passionate fellow, he seemed to have a lot on his mind. He was a sober alcoholic, and he meditated on the rosary as part of his recovery. He believed he had made a most amazing discovery, which he shared with me. Namely, that the person who originated the modern rosary, in about 1415 AD, was also an alcoholic. He regaled me at every meal. Then, after what turned out to be our last conversation, he handed me an envelope which contained the unfinished script. That night he died."

"I remember that," one student offered. "There was something in the paper. They were never able to identify him."

"Isn't this a little too much like a Victorian novel?" a young woman who wasn't Chloe asked. "Someone hands you a mysterious document then conveniently dies?"

111

"Exactly!" I rejoined.

The young woman, who had meant to carp, now basked in her insight.

"Then I drove to St. Louis, where I was supposed to retire, and where I read the script. At first, I didn't know what to make of it," I explained.

"Could you take off that hat?" another student asked, squinting as if he had forgotten his sunglasses. I took of my Cat-in-the-Hat hat, pulling it off by the crown rather than by the brim, so as not to mess up my neatly combed gray hair. It was not having the same effect it had garnered on the first day of class anyway. I stepped off the podium. Then I stepped off the stage and walked up the central aisle a few rows to be closer to my students.

"I finished the play myself," I continued. "So here I am with you today."

"But why were we all *encouraged* to take your course?" a student asked. She put air quotes around "encouraged."

"Who will be getting naked?" someone else chimed in.

One thing that always struck me about the cave paintings in southern France was how the artists used whatever they had at hand to create something extremely beautiful. What I had at hand was twelve Lutheran college students (down from fourteen), a magnificent Gothic Revival limestone church, and a script which had come sailing over the transom, so to speak. There was a long silence.

The same student spoke again, holding his hand as if to speak from the side of his mouth: "Chloe told me her parents are nudists."

They all looked at me, then at Chloe, who was fiddling with her boots. "She told me she has been running around naked her whole life," someone else added.

"That role...," I started, looking at Chloe, too. "That role binds the mother of our race, Eve, to the mother of Jesus, Mary, to the mother of Jay the alcoholic, Em."

Chloe stopped fiddling with her boots and looked right back at me.

"Anyway, I am a priest. I have no idea how to get a woman to take her clothes off," I addressed the class, arms up in an exaggerated shrug.

This got a pretty good laugh.

"You have to ask first," one of the boys offered.

I put my Cat-in-the-Hat hat back on. I got down on my knees in front of Chloe, who was sitting in the third row of seats on the aisle.

"Chloe...," I looked straight into her pale blue eyes. "Chloe, would you be interested in auditioning for the part?"

She did not answer. Silence gripped the room. I held my gaze. I do that sometimes while distributing communion, too. Still, she did not answer. She looked back into my eyes. Very few communicants risk that. At first, no one blinked, but what was the point of that? So then we both blinked.

"What the hell," she shrugged. She might as well have disrobed right then and there, there was so much raucous shouting and stomping and clapping from the rest of the class.

I passed a roadside sign in Iowa once that claimed that all of the rain that fell on one side of the sign drained into the Missouri River, and all of the rain that fell on the other side of the sign drained into the Mississippi. High school kids out drinking beer cannot resist pissing on both sides of the divide. It felt like we had just crossed some such imaginary line.

Though, of course, when the two rivers join at St. Louis,

the water all flows down to the Gulf together anyway.

‡

I noticed that one student, who I presumed was Marley [?], was in some kind of rage, chewing on a strap of his backpack and audibly tapping a heel against the leg of his chair.

"Okay. I would like the rest of you all to take the podium and tell us a little bit about yourself," I announced. This was Exercise I, from the *Improv!* pamphlet. "Who wants to go first?"

No one wanted to go first. I nodded at a lean, handsome young man with a carefully trimmed beard. He had an alert look in his eyes, and sure enough stood right up and went to the podium without further prodding.

"My name is Jay," he began. "I am a sophomore. It was suggested to me that I take this class."

At this, he made like his arm was being twisted behind his back.

"Good!" I interjected. Improv!

"I am glad we are all getting A's because my dad wants me to go to Drake for law school."

A little laughter.

"I played baseball in high school." He made as if swinging a bat. I nodded enthusiastically to show my approval.

"My parents are German Lutherans. My uncle had some choice words when he found out my professor was a Jesuit. Until I told him we were all getting A's—he went to Drake law himself. My sister has two kids and no husband. She can't seem to keep her pants on." This got a little less laughter; some of them seemed to know her.

114

"Is that what you want?" he asked me.

"That's good, Jay. Try falling off the stage as if you were drunk," I replied.

Jay began to stagger and spin and stumble, then fell off the stage in a heap. This got a nice round of applause.

"Who's next?"

The angry young man jumped up and rushed forward, taking Jay's vacated place beside the podium.

"My name is Marty," he spat out. So, Marty, not Marley. "I think you all know me. This is supposed to be a Lutheran college, so why we have a Jesuit teaching, I don't know. This isn't a real class—it wasn't in the catalog last year. I had an uncle who went to the University of Chicago for law. That's a *real* law school."

He glared at Jay. "If I had a sister who was a slut, I wouldn't be telling everyone about it."

Then, at me: "Do you want me to fall off the stage?"

"No, Marty. Please show me *being seated*."

He walked self-consciously to his seat, making some contemptuous gestures with his fists. The other students glanced at me nervously.

"Who would like to go next? How about you?" I asked, inclining my head slightly toward Chloe. She stepped right on stage with a confidence she didn't truly have yet, but seemed to be practicing for use later in life.

"My name is Chloe," she began with an affected accent. "My mother is French. I spend my summers in Paris with *Grand-mère*. I have a stepfather and a half-brother. He is *le petit* twerp." This followed by soft laughter from the class.

She continued, keeping the accent going, "People say my mom is a trophy wife because she is really beautiful and my stepdad is kind of old. He is a lawyer at Agri-World and travels a lot—all over the globe. I have two stepsisters, too, who are married and have kids. I am an English major. I have no previous acting experience."

Chloe had no tattoos or piercings, as if she wasn't quite sure how high in life she should aim yet. Her face had an ancient quality: when I looked at her, it seemed as if I could see her in the 14th century, then the 9th, then 500 B.C. She wore the same simple strand of jasper beads and the same stunning pair of cowboy boots that she was wearing the first day of class. The boots were tooled in long, interlocking, variegated rectangles.

"Give me more detail," I pushed for her to keep going. She looked unsure of what I meant, but tried anyway.

"My cat vanished when I was 14? I took this course because the chairwoman of the drama department *called my mom*, for Chrissake. I live in the dorms. I did not bring my teddy bear to college." *(Laughter.)*

"Like my roommate." *(More laughter.)*

"I had to drop calculus first semester. I have no car on campus, but I can go over to my parents' house anytime and get one of theirs." This last seemed like a veiled message for someone in the room.

"That's enough," I said. "Thank you very much. Could you lie on the floor as if you had been murdered?" She immediately fell (I thought she had tripped) into a very convincing heap of murdered flesh.

"Okay. Who would like to go next?" I checked the class list. "Cassie?"

Cassie was a Dominican-American — one of only eleven black students on campus — who was confined to a wheelchair by a childhood injury, information courtesy of the chairwoman and her wine. Cassie smoked incessantly, frequently where she wasn't supposed to, but people tended to cut her a lot of slack because of her handicap and because

116

of the school's poor racial balance. She carried around a little tin of cigarettes that she rolled herself the night before. How the chairwoman had known all of this, I wasn't sure, but it was a rather small school.

"No, thank you," said Cassie.

"Just go to the podium," Chloe said.

Using a side ramp, Cassie rolled up beside the podium.

I asked her to recite the line, "Who told you that you were naked," but before she could say anything, Marty lost it.

"What the hell?" he yelled. "Is this introductions or is this the casting? Why didn't you have *me* do anything? You said auditions were during Week 4!"

I walked over and got right into his space. "There has been a change," I said.

He backed down. I actually had had no backup plan if he hadn't.

"It isn't fair," he pointed out in defense. I agreed.

"Maybe you should drop," I suggested.

He muttered something under his breath that I didn't quite catch.

I turned back toward the podium, but it was vacant. Cassie had gone quietly back to her place! I knew in that instant that here was God. He, too, has this way of slipping away. Two students walked over to her, wheeled her back up to the podium, and stood beside her to keep her there.

"Okay, Cassie, tell us a little bit about yourself," I said.

"I'm taking this course because I need four more hours to graduate." She was looking at her knees.

"A little more," I prodded.

"I thought maybe I could help with props."

"That's good. Now...," I walked over and got my maroon Martin Luther sweatshirt, with the white letters stenciled on the front, wadded it up and put it on her head; it looked ridiculous.

"Now imagine that this is a turban covered with blue sequins."

She half-raised her arm in Benediction. It was devastating.

"You might make a good God," I nodded.

"Week 4," Marty muttered.

This had interesting theatrical implications. There was no way we could get Cassie's wheelchair on the little round stage we would use at the monastery. As Abraham, and in his turn, Job, pace the stage, back and forth in conversation with God, God, a black woman in a turban covered with blue sequins, would now have to keep up with them, swinging back and forth in a wheelchair off stage.

"That's all. Class dismissed," I announced.

Early dismissal checked any disappointment on the part of those who had not spoken. They grabbed their backpacks and headed out. Except Chloe, who stayed after class again.

"Are you also going for the role of teacher's pet, too?" I asked.

"I thought you'd like to know that Marty's parents are big donors."

"Got it," I nodded. The chairwoman had mentioned it. "How much money are we talking about?"

Chloe changed the subject. "We have some neighbors who are Born Again. They have a bunch of kids. One boy, Seth, is about 12. They believe that everything in the Bible is true." She paused for effect, then continued, "literally."

It took me a moment to realize what she was driving at. Mark 14: 50-52: *And they all left him and fled. Now a young man followed him wearing nothing but a linen cloth about his body. They seized him, but he left the cloth and ran off naked.*

"Do you think he would appear naked?"

Chloe saluted me, then turned sharply on her heel. Was she going for irony? She had just reached the door when she turned around.

"I actually already talked to Seth's parents," she hollered back, grinning. "We'll know by Tuesday."

Then she was gone.

‡

"Before we look at the script, we need to consider three things," I began the next class.

Marty was absent. That was fine with me. (As I was to learn, he was frequently absent.)

"The Divine Office, the rosary, and alcoholic drinking. I have decided that the best way to familiarize you with the Divine Office is to attend the Divine Office. Therefore, in two weeks, after Thursday's class, we will go out to the abbey and spend the night. You will be back on campus in time for your Friday morning classes."

This caused quite a stir; apparently they were still young enough to enjoy a field trip.

"I have 12 rooms reserved. Who can drive?" Both Chloe and Jay raised their hands. "Good. I can also drive. That should be enough."

"Do we need permission slips?" someone asked.

"No. We're in college, dipshit," someone else replied.

"We will get there in time for Compline at 7:30 PM. Then we will get up at 3:00 AM *(groans)* for Matins, and Lauds is at 6:30 AM. I'll show you where the stage will be, as well as the all-important offstage area."

This made it seem more real to them, I think: there really was a Trappist monastery out there, and we really were going to produce this play at it.

"Okay. The Divine Office," I continued. "This is 'office' as in the sense of duty; it is the duty of a monk to chant certain prayers every day. This is the main thing monks do. They also work, because they learned in ancient times that if you try to pray *all* of the time, you are apt to go crazy. The prayers they do pray vary from day to day, and they are different during certain times of the year, as well as on certain specific days. One such day is October 7th, the Feast of the Holy Rosary. That is the office that will be chanted by the monks behind our dramatic production. Please note..."

I paused.

"Please note..."

Everyone scrambled to get out their notebooks, which they had already grown used to not using.

"Please note that the version of the office we will be using has not been used by the Church since 1960 and has been *heavily* — underline that — *heavily*..."

They all underlined *heavily*.

"Has been *heavily* modified by the guy who gave me the script and whose tombstone is across the street from the abbey, bearing the name 'unknown.' It's a simple marker, paid for by the County, under a mulberry tree." I closed my eyes for a moment that I suspect was longer than I intended it to be. "Anyway, we can walk over there while we're at the abbey."

"Now, let's do some more introductions," I clapped my hands. "How about you?" I gestured vaguely at a group of young men seated toward the back of the auditorium.

One of the guys went to the podium. He had grown up on a farm. He lettered in swimming in high school. He worked a rural paper route on Sunday mornings.

"Imagine you are a chief of detectives," I prompted.

He imagined a trench coat, then he imagined a fedora, then he walked over to two imaginary detectives standing over an imaginary body.

"What have we got here, boys?" he asked. Whoa! This got an immediate round of applause.

"That was great," I said.

‡

"Next we need to cover alcoholic drinking," I began our next class. "Alcoholism is an ancient mystery—Alexander the Great, for example, had a wine goblet that held four quarts of wine. It was first noticed by Carl Jung, a student of Freud, that in certain people, for reasons that we do not understand, alcohol short-circuits their spiritual apparatus, so that for them, the pursuit of drink supplants the search for God. This wreaks a kind of havoc in the soul that is like no other. This reasoning became the cornerstone of Alcoholics Anonymous."

I paused to let them catch up with their notes, then continued. "In AA, one stops drinking, then develops an authentic spiritual life to fill the vacuum. Meditation is a part of this process. The man who handed the script to me was using the rosary as his meditation. He had somehow stumbled upon a startling insight: the monk who founded the Christian rosary, Domenicus Prutenus, had himself been addicted to drink. Questions?"

"How did he stumble across it?" Jay asked.

"He told me he had seen a translation of a short passage from Domenicus's writing," I answered. "I believe it was sort of an it-takes-one-to-know-one deal."

"Now, the rosary," I continued, waving off any follow-up questions. "Prayer beads, to quiet the mind and effect contact with God, originated with the Jains, and spread throughout the Hindu sects, and into Buddhism, Islam and Christianity. The first beads in the archeological record are from around 900 BC. In the West, they first appear among the desert fathers in Egypt, just off the main road from India to Rome. From there they spread to the islands off Ireland in the Dark Ages, then to the Irish mainland, and from there to the continent."

I wished the classroom had a map to punctuate these points. I started illustrating on the board instead. "Prayer beads, which became very popular, had been in Europe for perhaps 500 years when Domenicus added the life-of-Christ meditations." I wrote 500 years especially large.

"The prayer we repeat on the beads now, in the West, the so-called 'Hail Mary,' is taken from the Book of Luke. The words of the archangel Gabriel are combined with the words of Elizabeth, as reported by Luke." The board was now full, but none of the students seemed to be scribbling like mad in their notebooks.

"Are there any questions about the Divine Office, the rosary, or alcoholism?" I asked.

Silence. Pre-law was busy putting the finishing touches on an intricate mandala he had doodled in the margins of what appeared to be his math homework, Chloe was chewing on the edge of her thumbnail, and the entire back row seemed to have fallen either asleep or into a deep meditative trance. I finished anyway.

"We are going to interpret the meditations associated with the prayers of the rosary on a stage in front of monks chanting the office. Each meditation will be in three parts: early stirrings, the Gospel, and a contemporary scene. The monks will chant the office as they have been doing since 600 A.D. Our emphasis will be on the stage."

‡

Chloe remained after class again. She had a sort of cat-who-ate-the-canary look about her and fingered her jasper beads coyly. "According to the scriptures," she finally spilled it, her smile breaking out into a full grin. "Naked!"

Apparently Seth's parents' prayers had been answered, and their preacher had likewise signed off. I started to ask how exactly Chloe had managed to finagle Seth himself into agreeing to it, too, but she was already out the door, her invariable cowboy boots clicking down the hall.

Honestly, I had a little trouble assimilating this information. On the way back to the monastery, I stopped in a little tavern for a beer, something I almost never do. There was a sort of second room in the rear of the bar, and I noticed Marty back there playing video poker. He hadn't been in class again. He didn't see me.

I ordered a draw and drank half of it. Then it became clear to me: this was actually going to happen. The proctor was going to have fantods, and it was going to tear the bishop a new asshole, but *Rose Fire* was definitely going down, produced as written, nudists and fundamentalists united. I left, leaving the other half of my beer on the bar.

‡

Everyone was happy with the presumptive casting of Chloe = Eve/Mary/Em. There was no way any of the other females were going to take their clothes off in church.

Since Marty's father had indeed called the Dean regarding Week 4, to protect myself, I invited the chairwoman to a casting call and announced that the whole class would vote to determine the results. This was basically window dressing, as I already knew who I wanted and would orchestrate the audition accordingly.

We started the casting session with Job/Jesus/Jay. I selected two scenes: Jay staggering around drunk and shouting "Why me?" and Jay, having mastered AA, being admired by all of the women, which, of course, recalls the women following Jesus to Calvary.

Three actors tried out: Jay, Marty, and Pre-law. (The other pre-law, as Jay, of course, was also pre-law.) Time and time again, each in turn would stagger to the front of the stage and cry "Why me?!" as if they had been asked to take out the garbage. Marty actually handled these emotions best. He knew something like true rage, and his longing for approval was strong.

I panicked. Based on the audition, Marty should have the part. I called for a show of hands.

The result:

Jay — 13
Marty — 1
Pre-law — 0

Whew.

I announced, "Jay will play Jay. Chloe, I want you to work *closely* with Jay on his part." I figured if they worked closely together, Jay would eventually truly know rage, or something closely resembling it.

Marty was furious. "Shit," he spat. "I was better than Jay."

I didn't disagree.

"My dad is going to call the Dean," he added.

"He already did."

Two people tried out for God: Marty, who was still in a rage, and Cassie. For the auditions for God, I chose the

124

conversation with Job that begins Mystery VIII:

> *JOB and GOD are pacing back and forth together, as if in a search for middle ground.*
> JOB: Am I innocent? I am no longer sure.
>
> GOD: Have you visited the place where the snow is stored?

The essence of the matter here is that God cannot, *because of the nature of things*, answer Job's question. Not because he will not, nor because he doesn't know the answer. The answer is clear to all: Job is right. None of my would-be thespians got this. They all took the tempting attitude that God must be right, and that is how Marty played it: he shouted at Job in a complete rage. How dare *you* question *me?!* He fairly could have singed Job's eyebrows with his rage.

Then Cassie glided quietly up to the edge of the stage. She rolled alongside Job, as he paced back and forth, executing precise u-turns in her chair.

> JOB (Me): Am I innocent? I am no longer sure.
>
> GOD (Cassie): Do you want to see where I keep the snow?

Regretfully, gently changing the subject, with a touch of humor. Thus it was that we came to have a handicapped black girl God. Marty stormed out of the room. This time, however, it was fair: Cassie's God was much better than Marty's. After the production, much would be made of this in a review in the student paper, what an enlightened thing, etc., blah blah blah. The student reviewer also noted of Chloe, tongue in cheek, that it was "a good opportunity to see more of the sophomore class," *wink wink*.

Chapter IX

The day of the big field trip, Chloe was wearing her cowboy boots, as usual. She seemed to be defining who she was going to be, at least this decade, around these boots and the jasper bead necklace. She laughed easily. Nineteen. How old was Eve when she reached out *without hesitating*? Mary when she took a chance on a premonition? Mary Magdalene when she turned her first trick? Her father never returned from the wars, her mother was taken sick, she had little brothers and sisters at home to feed. Nineteen?

I had expected Chloe to arrive with a piece of expensive luggage; however, she had just stuffed a few extra things into her backpack. I could see a flashlight sticking out: probably her stepfather's idea. There was a little excitement in the air.

When we got to the monastery, the guest master was not in the office; the proctor was sitting in for him. When he saw his guests for the evening, I thought he was going to have a conniption fit.

"You must all sign the register! There is no talking after 8:00 PM! There is absolutely no smoking in the rooms! I will put the women and the men on separate floors! Do not come late to the office!" The proctor paused, then blushed deeply. "Do not put sanitary supplies in the toilets!" (This latter seemed to have to do with a recent plumbing problem.)

We left him muttering to himself. Clearly, he could see the potential here for much disarray.

Next to the office was the gift shop, where the monks sold inspirational books, religious jewelry, jam hand-canned by far-away monks, and caramels hand-pulled by far-away nuns. The local monks made wine for their own use, and they sold some in the gift shop, too. Visiting priests would buy a few bottles to use at mass. The gift shop was frequently unattended except for the occasional volunteer, and there was an honor box for leaving payment. Wine. Honor box. No one checking IDs. Any 19-year-old could figure this out; I'm still not quite sure how I myself did not at the time.

Anyway, we met in the cafeteria after everyone found their room. For supper: vegetable soup and homemade brown bread. All of the students sat straight in their chairs and no one complained. Afterward, we adjourned to the front lawn so the kids could smoke and get some exercise, I guess. There wasn't much else to do. Jay and some of the guys started tossing a frisbee. Cassie in her wheelchair gamely joined in.

"What are we supposed to do from 8:00 PM until 3:00 AM?" someone asked.

"Sleep," I answered.

They all looked at each other in puzzlement, then the bell rang for Compline.

‡

Compline is haunting, peaceful, and profound.

Oh men, how long will your hearts be closed,
will you love what is futile and seek what is false?

This must have had particular meaning for Domenicus,

128

who seemed, according to my erstwhile friend, to have found the AA solution to alcoholic drinking 500 years before AA.

You have put into my heart a greater joy
than they have from abundance of corn and new wine.

I went to bed at 8:00 PM, after Compline; I was tired. As I learned from the proctor later, no one else did. When I got up at 3:00 AM (for the monks, post-Vatican II, now chant Matins at 3:30 AM, not 3:00 AM as in our script), I went knocking on doors. I found everyone's room empty, from the south end of the third floor to the north end of the second.

When I got to Chloe's room, the last in the hall, I knocked harder. There was a muffled "yes?" I pushed the door open, and there everyone was. It is no mean trick to fit eleven people into a monastic cell (Marty didn't come): some were sitting in the window sills, some on the bed and on the floor, some standing in the bathroom, peering into the cell through the doorway. Chloe, it being her room, acted as spokesperson for the bewildered looking bunch.

"That proctor guy is *pissed*," she said, before I could even ask. I noticed several empty bottles of the monastery's finest in the waste basket.

"He caught us smoking out by the bell tower," Chloe continued.

"How the hell did you get out there?"

"Through the church. You just open the gate," Chloe shrugged. "But I'm pretty sure he thought it was tobacco."

"Christ," I muttered. I noticed the baggie of grass and some cigarette papers on the desk, poorly hidden under a copy of the script. Pre-law tried to subtly shift his weight to block my view.

"And a couple of guys were running around where those rows of iron crosses are," Chloe continued.

"The cemetery," I supplied.

"Right," Chloe spread her arms as if flying, to indicate what those couple of guys had been doing, then caught herself and pulled them back against her chest.

"Well, what did 'that proctor guy' say?"

"Get. Back. To. Your. Rooms!" she hissed through clenched teeth, lowering her voice and raising a shaking finger toward my face. I could even see the vein in her forehead bulging a little.

"What else?" Did I even want to know?

"The abbot. Is out. Of his mind," she bellowed, somehow again through clenched teeth, with both arms in the air. Actually, it was a pretty good imitation of the proctor.

Chloe was looking at me. Everyone else was looking at Chloe, trying not to laugh, then darting their eyes nervously toward the baggie on the desk, toward me, then back to Chloe.

"Well, Matins starts in ten minutes, so let's go," I shook my head. "Just take it in."

Bleary eyed, half drunk, a little stoned, and a little frightened, my eleven Lutherans huddled in the front pews of the dark church, as the feeble old cantor intoned *a cappella*:

Lift up your hands to the holy place
and bless the Lord through the night.

The ancient office of the night, sung in choir by generations of monks since about 600 AD, washed around them and mystified them and purified them and enraptured them. I think. Maybe?

Meanwhile, I tried to figure out what to do about the proctor. As long as he thought it was the abbot who was crazy, and not me, could I perhaps just do nothing?

‡

They actually went to sleep after Matins, some of them doubling up in their rooms, and it was impossible to wake them up at 6:15 AM for Lauds. By 7:30 AM, at breakfast, though, everyone was feeling a little better. The cook, Brother Terrence, kind of liked the kids and so served up a mountain of link sausages, a mountain of scrambled eggs, a mountain of hash browns, and an ocean of coffee. Not a monk's breakfast.

The proctor bustled in and made a beeline for the table where me and Chloe and Jay were breaking fast. I resolved to not speak a sentence that did not have the word "abbot" in it.

"Well, up bright and early, I see" he clipped, planting one foot on an empty chair.

"Yes, please thank the abbot for this wonderful breakfast," I replied, pouring more coffee and smiling more than civilly.

"You can thank Brother Terrence for that."

"Just carrying out the abbot's wishes, no doubt," I smiled harder. He still wasn't moving on, so I stood up and put *my* foot on *my* chair. He put his own foot down, then hastily put it back up again.

"They were running around the graves yelling 'woo woo,'" he accused, cutting to the chase.

"Just practicing *improvisation*, surely. *The abbot* was a master of it in his younger days." Was I laying it on too thick?

"*Stoned* might be more apt than *improvisation*." Chloe flinched. I opened my mouth to speak.

"I know," he interjected before I had the chance. "Abbot, abbot, *abbot*." Damn.

At that moment, providentially, the abbot himself joined us at the table.

"Talking about me are we?" He removed the proctor's foot from the chair, then sat there himself. Then, he poured himself some coffee. "Ah, Brother Terrence's finest."

"I was just explaining to the proctor the importance of improvisation in the play," I explained, sitting down myself.

"Ah, yes," nodded the abbot, turning to the proctor. "Could you run up to my office and get the printout for the farm manager?"

The proctor left in as much of a huff as he dared in front of his superior.

Chloe whispered, "Whew!"

"This is Chloe," I introduced her to the abbot. "She will be playing the parts of Eve, and Mary, and Em. And Mary Magdalene."

The abbot turned to Chloe, took both of her hands in his, looked straight into her eyes, and said, "I am *so* glad to meet you."

At this point, Jay said, "Whew!"

The abbot asked Chloe about her family, her major, how her classes were going, and her thoughts on the stage and the props and the costumes, and pretended to be interested in Jay also.

When the abbot left us, I said, "Whew!"

Young people get over hangovers so fast. Chock full of eggs and sausage, potatoes and coffee, we checked out of our rooms and headed back for campus, bright-eyed and with the indiscretions of the night before forgotten, the ancient liturgy ringing in our ears. Big stuff was afoot.

Marty had skipped our field trip, but I could have sworn I saw his truck pulling out of the cemetary parking lot as we left. Whatever.

Chapter X

"Alright," I said after everyone was seated, "today we will cover acting." It was Tuesday of Week 5.

A hand went up; it was Marty, back after his conspicuous absence. Why did he have to come today?

"I thought you said you didn't know anything about acting," he said, looking around for attention.

"I don't," I said. "I was a chaplain in the Army, then I taught at Catholic universities the rest of my life. When I was young in New York, I saw two plays: *Becket* on Broadway, and *Waiting for Godot* off-Broadway."

I stepped off the podium, stepped off the stage, then intruded way into Marty's personal space; he was in the third row. This put him in great physical distress. "Now what was your question?" I asked him.

"Nothing," he stammered.

"Good," I said as I retraced my steps back to the podium. Captain's bars meant something in the 101st, even if you were just a chaplain.

"According to Aristotle, Thespis is credited with introducing repertoire, in which an actor performs several characters, distinguishing between them by wearing different masks. In our play, you can see that Jay will be Job or Jesus or Jay according to whether he has ashes, a yellow ribbon, or a Harley-Davidson bandana on his head."

Chloe had gotten pretty good at repertoire already. When she was Eve, she easily radiated enough sexual energy to mother the whole human race. When she was Mary, she caught the tension between wanting to do God's will and having to put up with raising Jesus. When she was Em, she was all about drink.

And when she was Magdalene, she made you ache with the desire of the everlasting hills.

Cassie asked about segueing—how is God supposed to "segue"? I pointed out that segueing is what God does best.

I told the class to imagine that they had a TV remote control and that they were channel surfing between the Old Testament, the New Testament, and the present.

Cassie had noticed that, since she didn't change costumes, but instead always wore the turban with the penny-sized blue sequins, and since she was always offstage (since there was no way to get her onstage), she was less of a repertoire actor and more of an actor proper, and could thus exercise a little more Godly influence than was actually called for in the script. Fine with me.

"I want you all to feel completely comfortable wandering around the front part of the church, taking care of the costumes and props," I explained. "Note that *you cannot screw this up.* If you say things that aren't in the script, fine; if you forget to say things that are in the script, also fine. There is no need to memorize your lines—just carry a script!" This was *Improv! Carl Style.* I realized that I was yelling.

"What's the deal with that?" someone asked.

"It's like the Eiffel Tower," I improvised. "They never put the skin on it, so everyone can see how it is put together. It's the same here. We are not trying to fool anyone—we want them to see how the play is put together." That sounded pretty good.

"What is the purpose of the offstage?" someone else

asked.

"Imagine the production without it," I said. "Just the office and the stark events unfolding onstage. It would seem harsh and one dimensional. The offstage plants the production firmly in human nature (yours), and that is true faith: incarnate." I was on a roll.

There was a pause. I really have no idea what Lutherans believe. But a couple of students finally gave me a little nod, and INCARNATE became the banner under which we officially campaigned. (Unofficially: WHAT THE HELL?)

Marty grabbed his backpack and headed for the door. When he was safely out of range, he shouted back, "This is bullshit!" I couldn't deny it, but I was still going to put on this play.

Chloe stayed after class. "We're kicking up quite a bit of commotion around campus," she allowed.

I laughed. "Do you know the Aesop fable? A fly is riding down the road on a wagon thinking, 'I am kicking up quite a bit of dust.'"

"You are always hinting that there is more here than meets the eye," she said, rustling through the script, mock-looking for anything like more.

"There *is* more here than meets the eye," I insisted.

I let my eyes rest on Chloe. She was fresh, she was open, she was always laughing at everyone and everything, she was strangely vulnerable. Or maybe not so strangely. She was a spark from an ancient flame. Incarnate in an inquisitive, stable, fair-minded Lutheran college student. Maybe. I think.

"I think I can see the ancient flame from which you are a spark," I ventured.

She looked behind her—interesting, because that is where the ancient flame was.

"I don't see it," she said, rushing over to the fire alarm. For a moment I thought she was really going to pull it.

She walked with me to my car. It was the seventh time she had done so. She never hesitated to touch my arm or tie my scarf in public, like I was her uncle or something.

"Do you know what revenant means?" I asked her.

"No," she shrugged.

"You could look it up," I said, and she shrugged again.

"Do you want to go to the game? There is a basketball game tonight," she changed the subject.

"Do you play?"

"No," she shook her head.

"No, thanks," I said.

She shrugged her shoulders in a "hey, your loss" sort of way and skipped off—something you don't see too often. I tried skipping a few steps. I don't suppose she ever did look it up.

‡

My students were naturally divided between those who had any legitimate interest in acting at all and those who were just trying to get into law school and/or goofing off, plus Marty, whose motivation was apparently somewhat more complex. Of course, goofing off fit right into the script, which I pointed out to those who managed props and costumes, carried spears, and acted as understudies. This group became very enthusiastic and somewhat tight-knit. I suspect it was they who leaked the news to the student body that you got to see Chloe naked if you came to the play.

The next week I addressed this "flying squad," for thus they had dubbed themselves. "Our budget for costumes and props is zero," I announced. This tight constraint, I hoped, like the sparse pigment available near Lascaux, would explode into beauty.

The flying squad was amazingly resourceful scrounging costumes. For a Carthusian cowl they borrowed a brown hooded sweatshirt in 4XL from a maintenance man in the motor pool. They spent all one night making cookies, and then held a bake sale at a card table in the student union. Each $5 "monster" cookie came with a free ticket to the show. Of course, the show was free anyway. They were so proud when they presented me with what they bought with the proceeds of this sale: six yellow Harley-Davidson bandanas, three male and three female. Domenicus's high-collared jacket was sewn by the mother of one of the pre-law students. It was splendid. She had, at one time, taught Home Economics at the high school level and had been delighted for an excuse to get her sewing machine down from the attic.

Since the script called for the lector to wear the same jacket, and since I was the lector and the jacket was made to fit Jay, and was therefore way too big for me, she created a second jacket that was identical to it, only smaller.

The chairwoman of the drama department was on good terms with the chairwoman of the art department, which resulted in a student competition to design the giant rosary that would hang from the ceiling and frame the stage for the audience. It was to be retractable so that it could be cranked up into the rafters when not in use. The winning design used the oversized Christmas tree balls that hung, in season, on the huge evergreen in the center of the College of Martin Luther quad. These were a sort of iridescent metallic blue, and the finished product looked like modern sculpture. The artist was very possessive of her creation and insisted on being present when it was installed at the monastery.

The monks had a woodshop for their own simple needs,

mainly furniture and coffins. The carpenter monk constructed a round stage about five feet high and put wheels on it, so that it could be rolled into the church when we were rehearsing and rolled out when we weren't. The carpenter stressed to me that it was important to lock the wheels while the stage was in use.

Things were coming together.

Chapter XI

"My Mom says we should 'go do things together,'" Chloe announced one warm day in late March. A mom like no other. "To help with our 'theatrical collaboration.'" She made the air quotes, but her tone was not sardonic. I waited.

"So," she finally offered, "do you want to go play some miniature golf?"

"Sure," I nodded, swinging an imaginary club, which I immediately regretted. It's often startling, isn't it? How much life's small choices seem to add up in the end, their sum total both insurmountable and utterly inescapable. Looking back now, though, checking my math, as it were, there is still only one thing to say about it: I did want to play.

We drove over to Putt-n-Go in her car. I doubted the place would be open, but it was. The "Go" in Putt-n-Go referred to a small go-cart track adjacent to the links. The staff (one guy) knew Chloe and greeted her warmly. They were not busy; in fact, no one else was playing this fine March day, late in the afternoon.

On the first hole, Chloe shot 3 and I shot 1. On the second hole, Chloe shot 5 and I shot 2. She did much better on the third hole: she shot 2. I shot 1. On the fourth hole, I noticed an odd tension in the way she addressed her ball. It dawned on me that she was *really* trying.

So, on the fourth hole, Chloe shot 3 and I shot 7. After that, she seemed to relax. I continued to card 7's and 8's and 9's. She finished with a respectable 78 while I managed to finish with 103.

I had landed in the water hazard three times: once on the seventh hole and twice on the eleventh. When my ball squirted onto the go-cart track, I was penalized a draconian three strokes. I never did get my ball back from Ye Olde Mill on the fifteenth hole and had to play a new one, for which there was a two-stroke penalty and an extra charge.

This brought us to the nineteenth hole; if you shot a hole-in-one, you got a free game. Chloe, being low man, so to speak, went first; she missed. Then I teed up and made a hole-in-one. I gave her the pink free game ticket.

"Thanks," she said, tucking it into her pocket. "Do you want to try the go-carts?"

"It's almost dinner time," I demurred.

Chloe wanted to eat at the drive-in, which proudly advertised itself as "Not a Franchise!" I hoped it was on the historical register. Here, everyone knew Chloe. There was much honking and waving when we pulled in and, I supposed, speculating about who I was. The waitresses were, without a hint of irony, all on roller skates.

"I used to work here in high school," Chloe said.

My mouth began to water. Was I really going to get one last non-franchise chili dog in my time on this earth? A waitress rolled up, greeted Chloe, and tried to get a look at me through the windshield. I ordered a chili dog, a root beer float, and some extra napkins. Chloe ordered the Southwest Salad (a relative newcomer on the menu, I would venture), without the fiesta chips and dressing on the side.

"You wore roller skates?" I asked.

"Sure," she shrugged. "Of course."

The food arrived. Chloe dumped the entirety of her dressing on her salad and dug in, while I surveyed the utterly depressing contents of the little plastic basket on my lap. The hot dog was cracked, the bun dry, and the chili like paste. The microwave has ruined fine dining. The root beer float was okay, though.

A couple more waitresses rolled over and stuck their heads right into the car. Three guys, too, got the nerve to come over. Of course, they all wanted to know who the hell I was. "This is my friend Carl," is all Chloe would say.

"What do *you* like to do?" she asked me then, her segment of "doing things together" clearly over.

"I like to pray in the blessed sacrament chapel after Compline," I replied without thinking.

"Why?" she asked, after a long moment of conspicuous silence. I gave my shoulders a big how-should-I-know stage shrug.

"Can I come?"

"That is impossible," I shook my head. I should have said watching fish. Too late now.

"No, it isn't."

"Yes, it is."

"No, it isn't."

"The chapel is within the cloister. Only monks allowed."

"You are not a monk," she pointed out. I gave another big shrug.

"It's no problem. I'll wear a disguise." She was serious. I began to reflect on the numerous ways this could go south. For example, running into the proctor. On the other hand, one *might* be able to disguise her as a monk in a cowl.

"OK," I said. Chloe's conspiratorial smile lit up the whole joint.

After a brief discussion of "borrowing" a cowl, we headed for the monastery.

Chloe would remain in the car. I would slip into the laundry while everyone was at Compline, then leave the purloined cowl in a bush outside the rarely used south entrance before joining Compline myself.

It occurred to me that this caper might sink our boat, but how was I to resist Chloe's enthusiastic delivery of our unofficial battle cry: "What the hell!"

I arrived largely unnoticed, a little late for the office. Every time the proctor looked my way during Compline, I thought, "He knows."

Was there any possible upside to this undertaking? I supposed Chloe might bump up against some of the realities that were at work behind the scenes. But, being a 19-year-old girl, probably not. So, basically, the only reason we were going to do this was because I had already said "OK" and couldn't think of any way out of it. And our theatrical collaboration.

Compline was over. I walked around aimlessly until everyone went to bed, then walked out into the parking lot. There, on the hood of her mother's car, sat a beautiful young monk. She had managed to suppress her bosom somewhat, but there was nothing she could do about her hips, despite the ample robe.

"Pull the hood over your face," I suggested. "And hobble a little when you walk."

That helped. Sort of.

The dangerous part would be getting her down the hall to the chapel and back. If anyone came upon us in the chapel itself, Chloe would look as much like a monk as anyone else in the dark room, lit only by a single candle. Boldness, they say, is the essence of theft, and I figured that boldness would be the essence of this affair as well. We headed for the front door.

No one around. We went downstairs, and I let us into the cloister with my key, my precious gift from the abbot. No one around. We walked down the long hall. Moonlight shone through the Gothic windows, accompanied by the muted splashing sounds of water from the fountain in the interior courtyard. I was surprised that they had turned the fountain on so early in the season.

Through a very squeaky, very heavy wooden door, there was the chapel. No one around. We went in, we sat down. Being in the business, so to speak, I knew that that's it: go in, sit down, wait. Of course, Chloe knew nothing of such business. As soon as her eyes adjusted to the darkness, instead of remaining seated, she began to explore everything in the room, which wasn't much: the lone candle that served as the sanctuary lamp, the small tabernacle on the narrow stand, two barely visible icons on the wall, four long wooden benches. Having checked everything out, she returned to sit by me once more.

"*This* is what you like to do?" she asked.

I nodded.

"But what do you *do* here?"

"Well, first, I stop thinking, which took me about twenty years to learn how to do. Then I pray."

"Then pray." She took a reverent attitude such as Lutherans do, one supposes, when the minister prays.

"Dear God," I said. "Please help Chloe and me get out of here without getting caught, and please help us perform *Rose Fire* one time, for whatever reason."

We heard footsteps out in the hallway, coming nearer. We dared not breathe. But the footsteps continued down the hall and through another door.

After a while, Chloe whispered, "What do you mean, 'for whatever reason?'"

"That's what the guy who sold me that Cat-in-the-Hat hat said. You know, *'whatever,'*" I whispered back.

She shrugged.

"Let's see if we can get out of here without getting caught," I suggested.

We rose and moved slowly toward the entrance of the chapel. Her body grazed mine. Through the big wooden door. Squeak. No one around. Down the long hall. Moonlight. Splashing. No one around. Out the front door. Whew! No one saw us.

"What are you doing?" It was the organist, sneaking a smoke in the parking lot. "And why is Chloe in a cowl?"

Chloe looked kind of pouty. Her disguise had failed.

It is said that honesty is frequently the best policy. "I took Chloe to the inner sanctuary," I said.

"I hope the proctor doesn't find out," the organist shrugged.

"Unless you tell him, I don't think he's going to."

The organist, after a long pause, blew a perfect smoke ring. You used to see that in 'Nam.

"I never talk to the proctor. I don't think he knows I exist," he shrugged again. "I don't know where he thinks the music comes from."

The organist offered us his cigarettes. Chloe took one, I declined.

"You really look like a monk. No one would ever recognize you," he told Chloe. This cheered her up, although I noticed a certain contradiction in his remark.

"Timing is everything," he continued, segueing from discussing our escape from the inner sanctum to what he wanted to say about the production: that synchronizing the chanting with the dialogue on stage was of primary importance, in his opinion. Why didn't he come into town for a couple of classes and we could try a few techniques? Chloe jumped at the suggestion, and I suddenly felt a stab of pain so sharp beneath my ribcage, I needed to lean on the handicapped parking sign for a moment just to catch my breath. Whether this was a pang of jealousy or of indigestion, it was hard to say. But either way, it hurt.

"You know," the organist as we walked Chloe to her car, both of them smoking greedily, "I have a good feeling about this project."

"Me too," Chloe nodded. "I've never done anything before, really."

"I did something once," the organist remarked, blowing a somewhat more wispy smoke ring. "But it went south."

"I don't think this will go south," Chloe said. "Do you?"

"No," he shook his head.

I could think of several ways it could go south, actually, but why trouble their young minds? The organist closed Chloe's car door and Chloe drove away, leaving the organist and myself in the parking lot, and leaving my car at school. Never mind; someone would give me a ride in the morning.

Chapter XII

Thursday the next week, in the hall after class, after Chloe had yet again skipped away, the chairwoman mentioned that some of the other faculty, having heard that I was on campus, had expressed a desire to meet me. Accordingly, a luncheon was arranged in the faculty dining room, which was located just off the student cafeteria.

I arrived on the appointed afternoon immaculately dressed, as usual, in a black suit and Roman collar. We were to go through the cafeteria line on our own, then meet in the Crown Room, one of three private dining areas (the others being Thorn and Cross) partitioned away from the general seating. The cafeteria was swarming with students. A chalkboard announced the day's special: Chicken à la King over biscuits.

In the Crown Room, I found nine faculty gathered with the chairwoman around a single long table. As I was taking my plate of Chicken à la King off my tray, my sleeve grazed the white gravy. Great. I dipped a cloth napkin into the goblet of ice water already at my place setting, but as I was attempting to wipe the gravy off, I tipped over my ice water, which spilled into the lap of the small woman at my right, a professor emeritus of English and Drama. She yelped, and her pince-nez fell off her nose and dangled just above her lap, restrained by the black ribbon which attached this device to the blouse of her black dress. I could not remember the last time I saw someone wearing pince-nez. But they sort of fit the crabby old bitch, as events were to show.

The chairwoman vigorously patted my neighbor dry with a fresh wad napkins, but her efforts did not extend to getting the white gravy off my sleeve. It remained there all during lunch.

The chairwoman made the introductions: a theology professor, two English professors, two historians, and so on. I didn't even get a chance to tuck into my lunch (which had too many peas in it anyway) before the attack: "Wouldn't you agree that recent events prove that celibacy is impossible?" one of the history professors asked.

"No," I replied. "I think they prove that celibacy is very *difficult.*"

What a hostile lunch! A Jesuit on campus was apparently quite the event, and they didn't want to discuss anything except religion. Errors ancient and modern were brought to the table. The sins of the fathers were rehashed in some detail. And through it all, the chairwoman just sat there and smiled sweetly. She seemed to be amused. Was she getting even with someone? Was it me?

"Have you read our Code of Student Life?" a former math professor who had since advanced into administration asked. Everyone looked around knowingly at each other.

"Don't tell me you believe in the Assumption of Mary into Heaven body and soul." This the theology department speaking, and it wasn't a question.

"I believe that something happened," I countered.

Someone muttered "piffle."

They were just warming up. The emeritus professor on my right, who still had not completely dried off, pointed to the gravy on my sleeve, and said, "You should get that dry cleaned." Next, she took a cheap plastic rosary out of her purse and flung it on the table.

"Superstitious rubbish, wouldn't you say, Carl?" She made a point of not calling me "Father."

"No," I answered. "I would not say."

She raised her eyebrows, challenging me to say what I would say.

"I would say that it ties Christianity to one of the purest instincts, one of the earliest and most profound impulses to prayer."

She now rose; her pince-nez flew off again.

"Flapdoodle!" she sputtered, her spittle reaching my cheek.

"I would say that it chains you to the earth, while you reach for God."

"Balderdash!" she roared, throwing her elbow halfway at me.

This in effect ended the argument. People began making excuses and leaving. Most attempted to say something noncommittally polite: "Very interesting views," and so on. I was left alone with the chairwoman and my now cold Chicken à la King.

"Thanks a lot," I told her.

"I thought you did very well," she said, laughing gaily.

Good ol' Martin Luther hated the rosary, and it was heartening, I suppose, to find his spirit still strong at this, his namesake college.

"The faith is like a pearl. The church is like an oyster. Oysters are ugly, but without oysters there are no pearls," I said, not quite to the point.

"Professor Roundtree is a bit of a flibbertigibbet," was all the chairwoman said before she left, too, leaving me completely alone with my lunch in the empty room.

The organist drove over to campus on three successive class days, just after midterms. His hair was short, his glasses were a little thick, and he had a thin mustache. If he wasn't wearing a Trappist habit, I might have taken him for an agent at a second-tier car rental agency. In fact, he didn't wear his habit to class, and that is exactly what he looked like.

It turned out he had been pursuing a PhD in music theory when he became completely unglued and had to drop out of the program. There aren't many good jobs in music theory, anyway, so he said. He went to live with his mother and, when he was able, got a job cooking at a Waffle House. He began attending daily mass to get a little window of peace, where a young priest befriended him; eventually, he joined the Trappists. All this I learned via his self-introduction to the class. I later met his mother, who came to the show. She was so grateful her son had found his niche.

His main concern was timing. It was never going to work to have the dialogue onstage run parallel with the chanting in the background, as the author intended. The chanting and the dialogue would have to be interleaved. He came up with an ingenious device for achieving this effect: one of the extras hanging around the front of the church was given a small baton—very inconspicuous, unless you were looking for it. With this she was able, using the script, to cue both the choir and the actors on stage.

The organist urged the actors to listen to the words of the Psalms interleaved with their dialogue, so that the spirit of the ancient writers would inform their actions. He also entertained the class on the bagpipes and the tin whistle, though nothing he played in the classroom would prepare us for the electrifying effect these instruments were to have when played in the old stone church.

The organist seemed to see himself as a buffer between the choir monks and the acting troupe. Accordingly, he planned to participate in some of the screwing around in the front of the church — not even five feet from his organ, after all.

His main agenda, however, was that he wanted to add the theme from an old TV cop show called *Dragnet* (dah — dah dum, dum!) over the last scene of Lauds, where Chloe, as Mary Magdalene, lies murdered on the floor with detectives in fedoras looking on. Everyone was for it — Chloe was for it — but I was against it. I thought it was corny. The organist was very insistent: he turned to the students. "Chloe, lie down like a murdered prostitute," he directed. She immediately fell to the floor, murdered.

"Now give me three detectives in fedoras," he said. Three moved forward. Then he sang at the top of his voice, "Dah — dah dum, dum!"

"We'll see," I said.

"Perhaps the spirit does not speak only to you," the organist replied.

Right, then. "We'll see."

Chapter XIII

"Why don't you show Carl the house?" Chloe's mother suggested. I had been invited for dinner. The stepfather was in Europe, *le petit* twerp was at youth Bible study. Chloe just took me to her room instead. Jesus.

I apparently always look like I could use a cigarette — people who smoke are always offering me one (at Chloe's, everyone smoked except twerp). Being in Chloe's room, I think I should have been offered a carton. I have been in some strange places: jazz clubs, helicopters, firefights, the rotunda of St. Peter's in Rome. But I have never been any place more strange than Chloe's room.

Here was the famous teddy bear, along with about fifteen cohorts. Certificates and awards tacked up everywhere: graduation from third grade, second place in the 4 x 100 relay, confirmation in the Lutheran Church, Employee of the Month at the drive-in, pictures, pictures, pictures. And a riot of colors I seldom see: light pink and pale yellow and baby blue and peach. Ruffles on the bed clothes. A vanity. That was the first — and last — vanity I had ever seen in my life: white enamel and brass, with mirrors like a triptych. Did I mention the carpet? Cream, two inches deep.

Chloe sat on her bed and began painting her toenails; little pieces of cotton stuck out from between her toes. I lingered near the vanity. She was smoking some sort of cigarette whose marketing targeted women, but it spent more time in the ashtray than in her mouth. She offered me one, but I declined.

"Tell me a story," Chloe insisted, as if I were her father, and it was bedtime, and she was bored.

"When I was working in New York," I began after a moment. "One night after work, one of the waiters, Alan, talked his way over to my studio apartment. We were listening to music when suddenly he expressed himself quite frankly — going into some anatomical detail. As interesting as his proposal sounded, I shook my head. And wept. Alan embraced me, then left in a hurry."

Why on earth was I telling *this* story?

"Outside my building, he ran into a bunch of guys from Queens who were roaming The Village looking for queers. They beat him to death not one hundred feet from my stoop, then fled down the subway entrance. No one was ever charged. The restaurant was closed the day of his funeral."

Chloe was blowing on her toenails and considering them from different angles. Had she even been listening?

"Maybe you should just have let him," she finally said.

"It's a little late now," I pointed out.

"Or maybe," she seemed to reflect, "you shouldn't have." I, too, have always wondered if my so-called purity was worth it.

Chloe skipped off downstairs, her nail polish now safely dry. Assuming I had been left in her room by mistake, I waded cautiously through the carpet and down the hall. Chloe's mother met me at the foot of the stairs.

Dinner was decidedly not French. We had T-bone steak, mashed potatoes, and a lettuce salad with Russian dressing. For dessert: chocolate pudding topped with crushed Oreos and aerosol whipped cream.

"Do you want to have coffee with me in the morning?" I asked Chloe as I left. She was examining my hat instead of handing it to me; it is difficult for a priest to find an appropriate hat.

"Sure," she nodded, my hat now atop her own head. I had to take it off her myself to get it back.

‡

The Howling Dog Cafe, near the Martin Luther campus, catered to students and younger faculty, with a fair number of hip-for-Dubuque townies mixed in. We met there at 10:15 AM. It was rather busy, and everyone was leaning into their conversations. Neither Chloe nor I spoke for a while.

"I don't suppose I'll ever see you again," she finally said. "After the play, I mean."

"You never can tell," I ventured. Another long pause during which Chloe methodically rolled up a straw wrapper into a tight coil. "Does that worry you?"

"Do you know what it was like when I first heard about you, when I first heard about this play?" She didn't give me a chance to answer. "I knew, I *knew*, it was for me. People say they feel it in their bones. But it isn't in your bones. It's someplace else. It isn't anywhere, it's everywhere. Do you know what I mean?" She spoke with the certainty and sincerity of a nineteen-year-old hopped up on cappuccino and uncertain of whether they will be taken seriously.

"I do," I nodded. I did.

"And when I first saw you, I felt like I had known you forever," she added. "Like, you're *really* nice."

I looked at Chloe. "Nice" was the best compliment I had ever received. "Esteemed colleague" was tops there-to-fore. My mother used to call me "my little bunny."

"Is that what fate feels like?" she asked.

"No," I mused. Her face fell almost imperceptibly — if I hadn't been looking so intently, I would have missed it. "No, fate is awful, an inexorable juggernaut, which chews you up and spits you out."

Chloe perked back up and improvised some terror in the face of fate. "Right," I said. "No, the feeling you are talking about is God's will."

"You don't say," she quipped, rolling her eyes but sitting up a little taller in her chair.

"Never claim you know what it is. Follow it to the ends of the earth." Chloe attempted to improvise a response to this, with no luck.

"Do you want more coffee?" I saved her.

"Sure."

We had nothing else to do except sit there. Occasionally one student or another would come over and speak to Chloe about class or the play or whatever.

I like coffeehouses. I like the baristas' calls in the background. I like that nothing is really going on. When Chloe got up to get our third round of coffee, I watched the young men watch her walk up to the counter.

Looking around the Howling Dog, it appeared as if every female in the place was nodding her head in agreement. Here was Pharaoh's daughter, there the Fate that destroyed Job, and over there the harlot out on the streets at night. I was stunned by the incongruity — and by the congruity.

Chloe reappeared. "Did you tell anyone about your feelings about the play?" I asked.

She was caught off guard by this question and pretended to look for something in her backpack.

"My grandmother," she finally replied, quietly.

"And?" I asked.

"Put pedal to metal. Full stop. Love, *Grand-mère.'"
What, had she sent a telegram?

I smiled thinly at Chloe. She seemed far away, but she continued to smile confidently at me across the abyss.

"What do they have in common?" she asked.

"Who?"

"All of my parts in the play. What do they have in common?"

That was precisely what I had been trying to figure out. Why was I not trying to figure out Jay, who also passed through a number of complex characters: Abraham, Moses, Job, Jesus. It was because, I realized in sudden coffeehouse clarity, the rosary itself passed on the female side. That is what enlivened it, rocked it back and forth, to free it from the underlying stones.

"What they have in common," I said, "is that they are all women."

"And I am a woman," she nodded excitedly.

"No," I thought suddenly, "you are a little girl." I did not say it, but now I knew how to direct *Rose Fire*. My leading lady was but a girl, and she was imitating the roles women play. She would imitate holiness, and motherhood, and whoredom, and she would imitate them so well, none of us would even know the difference. If the essence of acting is acting, here I had it, pure and simple.

Suddenly, I missed the structure of my old life in Chicago: lectures to deliver, meetings to attend, deadlines to meet. Here I was sitting around a coffee shop trying to figure out what it was I was trying to figure out. In the company of this little girl who was on the greatest lark of her life — and was loving every minute of it, apparently. Maybe. Probably? I mean, it was pretty obvious that she had never been to Paris.

A young woman had just gotten her coffee and was headed for the door when Chloe sang out: "Jo Ann!" Recognizing Chloe, she immediately came and joined us.

"Carl, this is Jo Ann. We used to work at the drive-in together."

Jo Ann looked to be a few years older than Chloe, but not many. She was chewing a small wad of gum and wearing a folded bandana as a headband—it was a sort of domestic yellow one, and nothing like a Harley-Davidson bandana at all. Jo Ann, we learned, had just dropped her 3-year-old off at day care and was headed for her job at the plastic molding factory. She took no notice of me, as if she considered it just like Chloe to turn up with a priest in tow. Was it?

I listened as they caught up. Life had clearly dealt its cards somewhat more harshly to Jo Ann than to Chloe, at least as of yet: I gleaned that Jo Ann had dropped out of high school, married and divorced, and was now married for a second time. Chloe expressed appropriate concerns, asked about the baby, then told Jo Ann a little bit about the play.

"Why don't you and Joe come, and bring Emily?" Chloe suggested.

Jo Ann batted her eyelashes good naturedly and copped somewhat of a southern drawl: "I hate to tell you, honey, but you ain't near so pretty as your daddy made you think you are." They both dissolved into a fit of laughter.

On that note, Jo Ann headed for work, coffee in hand, swinging some pretty nice hips in faded jeans.

Chapter XIV

Chloe stuck around after class again, of course; precedent for her doing so had long been set. As usual, just giving the old Code of Student Life another yank. The chairwoman of the drama department walked in on us.

"All is in readiness," she declared, a little dramatically. "There is only one problem."

"And what is that?" I asked.

"What is the point of this play?"

I had an answer ready: "The author clearly intended to tear the skin off the rosary and let Mary and Eve and Magdalene out, from his heroine's radiant beauty in Scene 1, all the way to her dead body lying in coagulated blood, in Scene 15. The audience must leave with new eyes. The rosary is not an emblem of the reaction, it does not belong in the clutches of the rabidly obsessive and superstitious. It bears life. Chloe is its eidolon."

Chloe was standing a little taller, though perhaps not sure what *eidolon* meant.

"But what is the essence of Chloe's role?" the chairwoman pushed for more. Right.

"Chloe is playing three women," I began, then cleared my throat to buy some time. The chairwoman raised her eyebrows expectantly, a little too keen.

"What do you suggest?" I sighed.

"I have a dramaturgically risky proposal," she leaned in

and assumed a conspiratorial air. "Put two tall stools on stage, a spotlight on each. Everything else — completely dark. Sit and wait for your heroine to come. When she comes, listen to her."

"Okay," I said. Sure.

"Get a chaperone," she added, glancing at Chloe, who appeared to have tuned out after "eidolon."

There is one line in the Code of Student Life that makes a lot of sense: "The relationship is likely to be perceived in different ways by each of the parties in it, *especially in retrospect.*"

Chloe and I agreed right away on our chaperone: Cassie. When we approached her about what we were now calling "providing an alternative point of view," I had a carton of Chesterfield Kings under my arm to grease the wheels, as we used to say in the 101st.

And so, the day was set.

I was arranging the stools and the spots when Cassie arrived through the handicapped entrance. She rolled up to the back of the theater without speaking to me. I sat down on my stool in my pool of light. Cassie lit up one of my Chesterfield Kings in the back of the dark room. Surely *that* ran counter to the *Code*. By the light of her Zippo (a magnificent engraved one that she said her uncle got in 'Nam), I could see that she was wearing the sequined blue turban. Anyway, I enjoy buying them even if I can't smoke them.

We waited for what seemed like a long time, but it was probably only ten or fifteen minutes. A bar of light appeared as a side doorway opened, then all was darkness again. Who would appear? I could feel someone moving toward the other stool. She sat down, then we all waited. I was reminded of the time Chloe and I sneaked into the blessed sacrament chapel together.

Finally, she began. "Mom was born in Paris when *Grand-mère,* her mother, was 16. Mom has no idea who her father is. I was born when Mom was 16. I have no idea who my father is."

Had she rehearsed this?

"Mom began going to nudist camps with me when I was a toddler. She was looking for a husband. My stepfather was already married. He went to the camps alone when he was in Europe on business. That is where they met. There was a divorce. I have two half-sisters who are married already. I was ring bearer at my parents' wedding."

She paused.

"Now Mom and I spend our summers in Paris with *Grand-mère.* My little brother hates it."

She took a sip from a bottle of water that she had brought along.

"In Paris, *Grand-mère* takes us to mass every Sunday at Notre Dame. Back here we only go to church on Christmas and Easter, at St. Mark's." This the newer, modern-styled Lutheran church looming at the far edge of Chloe's parents' subdivision.

Another pause. I heard the distinctive click of a Zippo from the back of the theater. Chloe had sort of been addressing the empty seats. Now she turned to me.

"When I was in high school, my mom let me date older men in Paris, under very strict conditions, of course: itineraries, calling to check in, post-date debriefings. I met some people, danced in some clubs, ate at some restaurants. The oldest man I ever dated was 37." Pause. "He was a viscount."

From the back of the theater I heard Cassie snort, then start coughing. Then she quietly rolled up from the back of the room.

"You have no idea what getting established on this rock has cost, or what that looks like from outer space," Cassie accused. I saw that she was reading aloud from a cheap science fiction novel. Chloe laughed. Cassie rolled back to her vantage point, and we resumed.

"*Grand-mère* was quite a beauty in her day. Everywhere we went together, people seemed to know her. One summer, when I was about 12, my mom had to fly back to the States for a few days, leaving *Grand-mère* and me alone. As soon as mom left, Grand-mère stopped cooking and we took all of our meals out—breakfast in the coffeehouse, lunch at the sidewalk cafe, dinner in the most sumptuous restaurants.

"One night, after a day on the boulevard, we were at a restaurant where the maître d' called her by her first name and kept sending over wine. She began to speak to me as if I were someone else. A friend, maybe, or... not a granddaughter. She talked about art, and she talked about faith, and she talked about love. It all came out so fast, and it was all such a jumble, that I could not get it straight what she was trying to say. But the three were connected: love, art, and faith. So she said.

"Finally Grand-mère paused and looked at me for a long time. Like, really looked. 'I have lived a full life,' she said. 'Live a full life.'"

Chloe slumped over on her stool, then stood up and curtsied to the empty room. OK, then. She looked exhausted, but it was the sort of exhausted you would expect to see radiating from a silent film starlet draped across a fainting couch.

When we opened the double doors to the hallway, and the light flooded in, there was the chairwoman of the drama department. Cassie surreptitiously passed the book she had been reading from, the appropriate passage highlighted in yellow, back to the chairwoman.

"I get Chloe now," I said.

"Well, well," said the chairwoman.

You had to wonder if she wrote her own material: "Well, well." Really. And I never did "get" Chloe.

The four of us went to the student union for ice cream. Marty was at the union, shooting pool, but I don't think he saw us.

"I never did anything like that," Cassie said, addressing Chloe in her own French-styled accent and raising her little plastic spoon in an accusatory sort of way. "Did you?" Chloe waggled her eyebrows, and both girls broke into a fit of giggles so severe, half their ice cream had melted before they fully regained their composure.

‡

Marty had not been to class for five straight sessions. He did not return my calls or answer my emails. He was in danger of receiving an Incomplete, according to the policies of the Department of Liberal Arts. So I had the idea of tracking him down. There was no reason he should not receive the promised "A" if he would just *do something*. Also, I think I had the idea that, if we met on neutral territory, he might like me better and might even see the production in a more positive light.

I asked one of the male students where I might find him, and he suggested I try the Wagon Wheel, the bar just outside of town on the highway. Accordingly, I headed out to "the Wheel" one evening just before 10:00 PM. This was the same bar I had been to once before. The Wagon Wheel was an L-shaped building with a large parking lot. The short leg of the "L" was an ordinary neighborhood bar, while the long leg had a student flavor, with dancing and the added advantage that everyone could easily ditch their beer if the Sheriff came around checking IDs.

I spotted Marty right away. He was sitting in a booth and staring intently at something in the back room. I walked across the room to see if I could see what he was staring at. It was Chloe, who was dancing with some guys, apparently townies. There was a juke box. I decided to slip out unobtrusively, but Marty saw me.

"Hey, Shorty!" he yelled. Clearly he had had a few. I joined him in his booth. I was seated in such a way that I could not see the back room, but he kept glancing back there.

"I wanted to tell you that you are in danger of receiving an Incomplete," I said.

"Fuck it," was his answer.

"Well, if you would like to get the 'A' I promised everyone, it would be sufficient to show up and help the stagehands."

He looked at me with contempt. Or something. "Like I care," he shrugged at his beer.

It is notoriously difficult to reason with people who have had seven or eight, and that was the situation I found myself in. But I tried nonetheless: "I have nothing against you personally..."

"She's back there," he cut me off, pointing with one hand to the back room and making an arguably obscene gesture with the other.

I looked at Marty for a long time. He looked back. My first impulse was to grind him under my heel. This I resisted. "I think I hear my mother calling," I said absently, and left.

Chapter XV

The semester was slipping rapidly away. It was time for dress rehearsal already. This was on a Thursday; the show was on the following Saturday. No time.

We were out at the monastery again. A lot of monks had entered the monastery after the Second World War. After Korea and Vietnam, too, men coming back from the wars had sought the peace of the cloister. They seemed little concerned if a tractor wouldn't start, a window was stuck, or a doorknob came off in their hands. It was as if they accepted that, in spiritual warfare as in combat, nothing ever works like it's supposed to.

I, on the other hand, had been able to gain some control over my world. As an academic priest, and a Jesuit at that, I usually had all of my buttons sewn on, so to speak. This contrast, I could see, puzzled my students. They saw me, a priest in a tailored black suit, without a silver gray hair out of place, and then they saw the priests in the choir in rumpled habits, showing work boots below, a farmer's tan, their hair crushed by a seed corn cap. There were only a few possible conclusions to draw here, but which would be the one they drew?

When we were all gathered in church for rehearsal, and before I could say anything, one of the monks—Fr. Javier, the suspicious—spoke out: "Fr. Carl, what exactly are we trying to accomplish here?" Well, at least someone was paying attention.

I dropped my script, and its binder clip popped off. Several students rushed to help pick up the pages and get them back in order, and to show that they were on my side.

What's up with being a monk? It looked to me like they drove each other crazy, that the path to holiness available to them was to get over the fact that the other monks drove them crazy. Maybe that's the way it is with us all. I gave Javier what, in my brief tenure as a professor of drama, I had come to refer to as The Long Stare. It worked on Marty, and it worked on the proctor. Would it work on Javier?

I told again how I had come to have the manuscript and about the snowstorm. This caused a little distraction, as the monks began to reminisce again amongst themselves about the storm. The organic grade of their cattle was lost yet again in the retelling. I added a detail which I thought might appeal to the skeptical Javier: how the author's hands had trembled when he handed me the script, how the fire in his eyes flared up for a moment, a moment which quickly passed.

When Fr. Javier spoke again, it became painfully apparent that I had over-sold it: "So you just humored this guy for your own amusement, to relieve your boredom during the storm, and now you find yourself caught up in his story and don't really know what you are doing." Was it a question?

I don't think my students had ever heard adults speak to each other like this. The Trappists have always had a certain reputation, that some of them are pretty sharp. I was getting angry. Perhaps Fr. Javier was trying to make me angry.

"What we are doing is putting on a small dramatic production with the office as the background," I began. "But the question has been raised, 'Why are we putting on a small dramatic production with the office as background?'"

Fr. Javier took a few steps forward, as if to say, he would be answered. Between his raised cane and his aggressive stance he managed to radiate: "What are you doing in my monastery?" "What is all this crap?" and "When do we get back to the peace I sought when I came here?" without actually saying anything.

I tugged at my Roman collar and addressed him: "Well, Father..."

He took another step forward. "Don't give me any of this 'Brotherhood of the Cloth' crap," he fairly shouted. His unruly eyebrows flared. I always keep mine neatly trimmed. But the only answer I had to the gnarled cane he shook in his fist was my rapier wit. Well, the Jesuits are forever getting into it with the scholarly Dominicans, but I don't ever recall of hearing of a Jesuit and a Trappist duking it out.

"Javier, I...," I began.

"You can call me Joe," he replied.

"Joe, I...," I tried again.

"What's your name?" he demanded.

"Carlos. Could you restate the question?"

"Yes. What in the hell are we doing here?"

"This is a dress rehearsal...," I began.

"I know that, stupid," he replied, upping the ante a bit, a little spittle landing on my clean suit.

"The abbot...," I tried another tack.

"The abbot is a fool," he countered, cutting me off at the pass.

"If the nudity offends you...," I retreated.

"Nudity doesn't offend me!" This he shouted so loud the echo nearly rattled the pews.

There was a stunned pause.

I summoned the authority formerly vested in me by the

101st Airborne: "Look, Joe, I will tell you what we are doing here if you will shut up and listen. But keep in mind that this play is being performed Saturday night, whether or not you like it, and whether or not you are in it." In a lot of outfits, the chaplains tried to be nice. Not in the 101st; we were constantly in combat.

This seemed to blunt his attack, and he sank back into the safety of the other monks. My students were left wide-eyed by this exchange; they seemed to be hoping it had been staged on purpose, that none of it was really happening. It looked to me like you didn't really have to be in your right mind to be a monk, you just had to be able to act convincingly as if you were. Perhaps it is so with us all. Creative work has a natural manic/depressive cycle. One day genius, the next day crap. So it was with producing *Rose Fire*. Fortunately, that day I was thinking genius.

I looked at Chloe, who was taking all of this in. The adrenalin coursing through my veins seemed to clarify my vision; I had noticed that in combat, too.

Honesty is frequently the best policy, but would it do here?

"Alright. I fell asleep watching a tank of fish in a nursing home. I had a dream. A woman was standing before me stark naked, beckoning. It seemed as if she wanted to show me something. Then the woman and I heard someone walking along whistling, but we could not see him. It was a familiar air, but neither of us could place it.

"All of a sudden we were in front of an angry mob. No curse was too vile for them to hurl at us. The woman's nakedness drove them mad. They rushed at us, but we were suddenly pulled out of the scene and reappeared on a long, low marble bench, set in a vast expanse of sand. We could see the cosmos spinning all around us, galaxies colliding. I noticed some rosary beads on the bench beside me and picked them up. The entire cosmos stopped and waited; the woman stopped breathing. So, I began to pray, and the whole cosmos began to move again, who-knows-what happening in its depths.

"I was startled awake by the clatter of buckets; a young woman from the service that maintained the fish tanks had come for the monthly filter cleaning and water change. Later that day I had the sense that I now knew *why* I was doing what I was doing, although I would be hard put to explain it to anyone else. But I still didn't know *what* I was doing, if you know what I mean."

No one did seem to know what I meant; most of my students avoided eye contact. Fr. Javier's cane was resting on the ground once more, though, so that was something.

"Why does anyone *do* anything anyway?" I asked the ceiling, continuing my attack.

Now *I* was beginning to shout.

"Why have you been singing the office at the edge of the steppe since 1848?" I demanded. There was a long pause. I took a deep breath before continuing with the *coup de grace*: "I have come to believe that certain pictures were beamed to Earth in 1483; a humble woodcut artist recorded them and was never heard from again. Now we are beaming a version of this work back into space to acknowledge receipt of the pictures, and to say thank you for them. Then we, too, will never be heard from again." *Touché!*

Fr. Javier re-emerged from the safety of his monks and stood in no-man's land.

"Well, then," he said. "OK."

Cheering broke out in the ranks of the students and the ranks of the monks, as if on cue.

Dress rehearsal went OK. Marty wasn't there, which helped. During a break, the students went to smoke out by the old bell tower. Returning with the pack, Chloe remarked, "We met this guy. I don't think he was a monk, though."

I glanced out to the bell tower, but whoever it was, he was gone.

The performance was a little rough. I had trouble getting the Greek chorus to assume any moral authority; they just wandered over to the stage like they were going to look at some roadkill or something. Synchronization was a problem, as the organist had foretold, and the result was a sort of gap-iness, like a loosely coupled train starting up. The young Seth was there with his father.

But the chanting was gorgeous—chanting the office is, after all, the main thing that monks do. The changes to the office that had been made, they sang without batting an eye. "If this is what the abbot wants, this is what the abbot gets" seemed to be their attitude. The soaring voices in the old stone church crashed around our crude wooden stage like it was a boulder near the shore of the sea.

Chloe did not undress during dress rehearsal, although the boys kept chanting, *sotto voce*, "Take it off! Take it off!"

"Don't worry," she winked at me. "Saturday."

Like Chloe, Seth did not disrobe at rehearsal, but his father reaffirmed he was going to do it, because it said so in the Bible. Although I thought his father's worldview bordered on the crackpot, it certainly enriched our little undertaking.

In almost every lull, Seth's father struck up a little conversation with the organist, and chatted with Chloe, who was, of course, his next-door neighbor. He didn't seem to be paying attention to the play at all, aside from the bits surrounding the Alcoholics Anonymous angle; his small church attempted to reach out to the downtrodden. He was a cattle buyer, though it wasn't quite clear to me what this entailed. But he immediately made himself comfortable and was, in effect, our only audience at dress rehearsal — everyone else was in the play.

And, to my amazement, he began offering helpful criticism. For example, he thought the cast should pass out programs to the audience after they were seated, instead of at the door. I couldn't see the difference, but we went with it. Segueing from the Old Testament to the New Testament to the present was sometimes a blur, he reported; perhaps he had been paying attention after all. Or perhaps not. He suggested background music (theme music, as it were) to make it clear where we were situated timeline-wise, an idea that the organist immediately took up. Fortunately, he really could improvise.

Seth himself could be called nothing but "well-behaved," sitting at attention in a pew until cued to action on stage, then promptly returning to his seat.

At one point, the proctor came into the church. The abbot quickly cut him off at the pass, sending him off on some complicated errand. Of course, having the first and only rehearsal two days before opening night exposed us to a lot of potential problems. But I considered that the rough quality of our production, like the rough quality of the original woodcuts from Ulm, would only add to its beauty *as seen from outer space.*

Chapter XVI

Rehearsal ran late, but no one seemed to care or be particularly surprised. The abbot decided to move Vespers into a side chapel at 5:30 PM, so we could continue rehearsing. When we were finally done, the monks adjourned to their rooms to change into mufti, Seth and his father departed in a rather surprisingly flashy sports car, and the rest of us waited in the parking lot. When the monks came out, they looked like farmers dressed for a funeral. We headed for a Japanese restaurant near campus in three cars and two vans.

I seated them by alternating monk/student/ monk/student, a kids-in-jeans monks-dressed-as-farmers-going-to-a-funeral blend that went well with the faux Japanese décor. It was interesting to see what passed for Japanese food in the Heartland. Nothing would do except everyone try chopsticks. And sushi, which none of the monks and only two of the students had ever had before. It proved to be a nice icebreaker as everyone advanced their feelings *vis-à-vis* eating raw fish.

I ordered sake for everyone; I was hoping they would not check ID's, and since we were in a private room (and the wait staff didn't speak much English), they didn't. Was I the only one who noticed that the help was mostly Mexican, not Asian? The organist declined sake; a bottle of mineral water was found for him. The rice wine really broke the ice.

During a lull in the conversation, Chloe asked loudly,

"So... do you guys really never have sex?" I kicked her under the table.

"Ow!" she muttered, wincing visibly.

I was about to change the subject, when Fr. Javier took the matter up: "No, that is a very good question, Chloe."

The chef was at the table, his knife flicking rhythmically through some brilliant red tuna. He clearly understood English better than he had been letting on.

"Celibacy is a very difficult discipline, the pursuit of which often ends in tragedy. For many it takes years to master. Many others never can. But if you can master it, it takes you to a very high spiritual place," Javier explained.

"What would a very high spiritual place be like?" asked Chloe, leaning in. She did not use air quotes, but they were in her voice. Meanwhile, there was a lot of low comedy as people attempted to eat the chef's proffering with chopsticks. Failing to get an answer to this, Chloe (and the sake in her) got a little more aggressive.

"So what the hell is the rosary all about anyway?" she asked.

Javier looked around the table to see who might take up this question. I signaled the waiter for more wine. When Javier caught my eye, I signaled, "Hey, Joe, it's all yours." There were some lively conversations going on at the long table. Monks were convincingly feigning interest in student life; students were likewise convincingly feigning interest in monastic life.

"Well," Javier finally answered Chloe's question, "when you start out, it is like knitting or playing cribbage, a diversion. Then, if you stick with it, which most people don't, it starts to change. Your hands will long for your beads, your spirit will long for quiet to say them."

Javier looked around at the other monks—he knew

them all well, knew how far each fell from the ideal. Some of them were quite damaged, by the war, by their parents, or just by life. Each had gained enough humility to make it as a monk anyway.

Javier continued, "For years you fight distraction, then you give up. Then the distractions let up and the ones that are left are kind of interesting."

Chloe was paying Javier close attention, whether out of her own personal interest or because of her part in the play, I could not say.

"Then, one day, something out of the ordinary happens. It is different for everyone, but something happens to each that will pretty well convince them for the rest of their lives that there's more here than meets the eye. You're hooked. You follow them anywhere, you take them everywhere."

"Then what happens?" Chloe asked.

"Nothing," I thought.

I was about to jump in—I, after all, was a Jesuit. But Javier put his arm in front of me, as if to say, "You already had your chance at this question."

"Then you die, like everyone else," he concluded. "But you die with a fire inside you that goes to join the big fire." He laughed heartily at his own rather un-Christian conceit.

"But then what?" Chloe asked.

Everyone was impressed by the restaurant except Chloe, who claimed to have been to better restaurants in France many times with her mother, and Javier, who had served in Asia during the war and had been married to a Vietnamese woman; she had been a phenomenal cook before she died in childbirth along with their child.

Some of the monks, now tipsy, were getting on the abbot's case about his homilies (the abbot had not come to dinner). I said I thought his hortatory supererogation had a certain sibylline opacity. Chloe kicked me hard under the table—I almost knocked over my water.

"What the hell?" I muttered.

"No one knows what you're talking about," she hissed.

"Well, they should," I hissed back, brushing drops of water off my sleeve.

Chloe, who had been denied twice in this conversation, rolled her eyes toward the ceiling, as if to say, "Perhaps you would like it better if the children sat at the card table." Why could she not just show a little gratitude? After all, wasn't it still me who materialized out of nowhere, bearing the big part, her chance of a lifetime?

A lively discussion about football started up, then we talked about basketball. Then the natural progression to baseball. The Cubs, it seemed, after a rebuilding year, might have a shot at the pennant, though it was premature to say at this early date, etc.

What next? Chloe was a little drunk and making goo-goo eyes at everyone. I wished she wouldn't do that. The soup arrived at the wrong time, but no one noticed except Javier. He spooned right in. What the hell? Soup!

As I looked over this improbable bunch (some of the monks were in their 80's, most of the actors were 19), drinking rice wine and trying to eat sushi with chopsticks, while the chef's knife flashed (I was pretty sure now *he* at least was Japanese), a powerful feeling stole over me. I could not name it. How lost we all are here. The improbable nature of what we have to hold on to. The faith required to get even a little faith. And how grace carries us along anyway. Chloe: the grace of being beautiful. Javier: the grace of being old. Fr. Javier was lighting Chloe's after dinner cigarette for her. And me? The grace of being rootless. The Jesuits knocked themselves out trying to root my life in Christ, but, of course, being rooted in Christ is precisely to be rootless. It's in the book; I looked it up.

I tapped a chopstick to the edge of my glass for a toast, and everyone fell silent. Raising my glass, I declared, "To Domenicus Prutenus and whoever did those woodcuts in 1483!"

Chloe responded: "Hear, hear!" Then everyone chimed in: "Hear, hear!" "Hear, hear!" "Hear, hear!"

Everyone likes to shout "Hear, hear!"

Soon it came time to compute the tip. The bill was $457.21. Eighteen percent of that would be $82.30. Management would probably skim at least a quarter of it, and since the help was probably undocumented, an even half. Ten percent for the busboys. Four people actually did anything (not counting the chef, who was surely one of the owners). For each waiter to get at least $50, I figured, I would have to leave $450, which is what I placed on the table, in cash: four $100's and one $50, in plain site, so the help could count it before management got a hold of it.

"The last of the big tippers," noted Chloe, her hand suddenly on my arm. I couldn't tell if she was being sincere or sarcastic, or if she was just tipsy. It suddenly occured to me that shortly after graduation, Chloe would probably marry some Lutheran who had inherited a car dealership and have five children, becoming a little broad in the beam, as they say, as she otherwise aged gracefully, gradually becoming her mother. This thought mingled oddly with the aftertaste of raw fish and the smell of grilling pineapple.

As we walked to the cars, Marty's Jeep pulled into the parking lot, as if he had gotten the wrong time for dinner. But when I spotted him, he took off again.

Now we had to figure out how to get 27 people, most of whom had drank too much, home without anyone getting a

DUI. The only two we were sure were sober enough to drive legally (0.08 BAC) were me and the organist. It was like that riddle where the farmer with two chickens and a fox is trying to cross a river in a kayak which will only hold him and one animal (and, of course, never leaving the fox alone with a chicken). Take the fox over, come back and get a chicken, bring it over, *take the fox back*, bring over the second chicken, then go back and get the fox.

The monks had two vans. The sober brother would take six monks and one student. The student would bring back his little sister, who had a learner's permit and was always itching to drive; they, in turn, would take four students home. The sober monk would come back and get the rest of the monks, then come back in the morning with someone else to get the other van. Everyone else would pile into my car (and I do mean pile) and rendezvous at the student union the next morning to come get their cars.

I set off with a car full of silly, drunken, satiated kids who now surely felt attached to some higher calling (hear, hear!). Six in back and three in front with me. There was a little playful groping going on, I gathered from their giggling. I dropped students off and wished students good night, and the last person in my car was Chloe. Imagine that.

On the way to her house, I stopped for a few minutes at a little roadside park that overlooked the town and the river beyond. We could see from the lights how the town hugged the river. Then we moved on.

"So," she said, "I suppose you think I am going to marry someone who owns an insurance agency and have five kids."

"To tell you the truth, I was thinking along the lines of a car dealership," I said.

"In high school, I was County Corn Queen, but only

because the prettiest girl got strep."

I wasn't sure how to respond to that, so I didn't say anything.

"Why are you being so mean to me?" she asked.

I pulled into her driveway. She had the door open, and was skipping toward the safety of her porch light before I could answer, leaving me, the improbable rosarian, alone with my thoughts.

Chapter XVII

I drove in the country for a while before taking myself home to the monastery, repeating and revisiting in my mind the evening and the little party, which I concluded had come off well. In my taking Chloe home, however, I found myself wishing for a chance to revise. Suppose that Chloe had reached over and tousled my hair as we drove along together! I have always used a little mousse, so this attempt at kindness actually would not have worked out very well for either of us. Chloe would surreptitiously wipe her hand on my front seat and take out a cigarette but be unable, in the dark, to find her lighter.

"There is a lighter in the glove compartment," I could tell her.

Rummage, rummage.

Suddenly, shriek!

"What?"

"Your maps are in alphabetical order! Arizona! Colorado! Delaware! Florida! Iowa! Kansas! Missouri!"

Pause.

"Do you want to know the rest of my secrets?"

Another pause.

"Sort of."

So I wade in. For one thing, it is a little weird being a priest. God is a little hard to relate to. Another thing, when I was teaching, I always used to eat orange marmalade for breakfast, on an English muffin. When I moved out of my apartment in Chicago, I threw out eighty-nine of those nice little marmalade jars. A third thing: my middle name is Frampton. That's my mother's maiden name. I don't like it and have never used it.

At that point I could imagine Chloe saying, "Pull over, Carl."

I would stop on a tree-lined street, half a block from the nearest street light. The moon would play off the dew on the well-manicured lawns. An abandoned tricycle would sit in a silent driveway. I am getting quite good at this directing thing.

"Let's do this," she begins. "I will tell you three things, then you will tell me three things. Then you can take me home."

I like the idea. "Fine."

We both sit and think for a while about what we are going to say, until the script is perfect.

CHLOE: I'm going to give it everything I've got. I'm not sure why.

CARL: In the dark ages, some Christian missionaries appeared at a Muslim court asking to be heard. The bailiff asked the sultan, "Shall I just have them beheaded?"

"No," said the sultan. "Call my wise men."

The wise men deliberated for some time, then sent back word: "Most exalted Sir, if these men presume to know anything, perhaps you should hear them out. Because, to tell you the truth, we have no idea where we came from or what we are doing here."

That is right out of the banned works of Fr. Anthony de Mello, S.J. Chloe would nod so as not to use up any of her turns replying.

Both of us would think some more.

CHLOE: I have never ever met anyone like you in my entire life.

CARL: An Indian officer was to be shot; they granted him a last wish. "I want to see my homeland again," he said.

So they took him to the border. He looked out over the mountains and wept. "Now I am prepared to die," he said.

But the Pakistani officer in charge of the firing squad said, "Wait a minute! There's been a mistake. The border is ten miles farther on."

More de Mello.

Here, I would probably begin to cry. It would surely take Chloe a while to get her mind around that. I started to wonder if de Mello might be a little too deep for Chloe, but I did not revise again.

Next Chloe, too, would begin to cry. I would start the car and find my way to her parents' house, between the teardrops. They would not have waited up. She doesn't say goodnight; neither do I. She skips to the safety of the porch light, much the same as she actually did, but this time pauses to look back at me watching, engine idling, and she waves before she digs her keys from her purse and disappears into the house. She flicks the porch light off, leaving me to watch the dark house for a moment more. We never get to the third thing.

‡

I took the blacktop back to the monastery through the dark fields. Back at the abbey I picked up my rosary beads and looked out on the quiet courtyard—just the old fountain splashing. My hands were so grateful to have the beads. My being longed for the words, which my mind began to turn over, "Hail, full of grace..." The moon, nearly full, came out from behind a cloud and flooded the courtyard with light. I passed into the realm where words are of little use. Not until my fingers found the end of my beads did I stir.

I was not the same man who materialized out of a snowstorm, just before they closed the road, some sixteen months ago. I was still a priest. Still a Jesuit, albeit one put out to pasture. I still knew as much paleography as I ever did. I still owned five black suits. I still remembered the prices from the menu at the Succulent Pig: half rack, slaw, roll, drink $7.27. (It was kind of an expensive place.) But now I was about to embark into the metaphysical unknown, to carry out the vision of a passing depressive whose remains lay in a pauper's grave across the road, who will be forever remembered as "unknown."

And then? I thought I probably already knew how this story was going to end. My erstwhile friend had mentioned to me a manuscript at the monastery at St. Albans, Trier. Had he *been* there? Either way, Domenicus's proctor had instructed him to write an account of his life, which he did. Now it was at the public library, Stadtbibliotech Trier, in the medieval manuscript collection. I already had my tickets; my plane left early Sunday morning.

Tomorrow there were a thousand details to attend to, then Saturday was the big day. I fell into a fitful slumber. I dreamed that I was sitting on a long marble bench in the middle of endless sands. Chloe came and joined me on the bench; she had just taken a shower and was wearing only a giant bath towel. Next to join us was an emaciated, nervous man who looked like a medieval clerk. He was wearing Domenicus's tight fitting jacket from the play. He was obviously quite taken by Chloe's dark hair.

Then across the sand came a shadowy figure that the three of us could barely make out. All we could see was that it was a small, grey woman of about 50, dressed in rags, and covered in printer's ink. She carried a small carving tool in her hand. It was clear that she had been ravaged by the plague.

When the bell rang, I awoke and shuffled to Matins with the rest. In the stillness of the night, these monks have been singing the office for ages. If it was nothing, it surely would have died out long ago, no? It was like an overhand knot: you slide the rope through the knot—you have different rope, but the same knot. The monks die, new ones appear, but the office is the same. The monks stay up after Matins and study, but I went back to bed. I slept through Lauds, Mass, breakfast, and Prime, and was finally awakened at about 10:00 AM by the clanking and whir of an old lawn mower somewhere outside.

Chapter XVIII

The prior stopped me in the hall Friday morning; it was rumored that he really ran the place, that the abbot was an ineffectual figurehead.

"What exactly is happening tomorrow night?" he asked. I could understand why everyone kept asking me this question; I sort of wondered, too. But the prior seemed to have a more urgent agenda. It seemed that the bishop had heard certain rumors while attending the local Area Interfaith Council on Poverty and the Homeless. Monseigneur had called from the chancery to inquire.

"We are putting on a concert and morality play," I replied.

"No nudity?"

"Everything is scriptural," I assured him, ducking my chin and lowing my voice half an octave. My knowledge of Latin had taught me a little rhetoric: *ignoratio elenchi*.

"Right, good," he clapped his hands together, glad to get the matter off his desk. "Everyone thinks a monastery runs itself! Are you kidding me? Who buys the cattle feed? Who files the tax exemptions?!" He hurried off down the hall, the shuffle of his sandals on the worn flagstones echoing softly off the stone walls.

I would be in Germany long before the inevitable inquiry was convened. I myself had served on inquiries. It takes about three months minimum to select the inquisitors, frame the issues, find a venue, establish a budget, and so on.

There is no way this little diocesan inquiry would have enough money to fly me back from Germany to testify. Instead, I would be asked to respond in writing to certain questions they had. Whatever.

I admit that, originally, I was just humoring the guy. We were snowbound together. I had been reading St. Francis de Sales, for whom how one treats difficult people is the litmus test of one's spiritual condition. I fancied that I knew something of the rosary myself. And now I was caught up in events which had moved me far beyond my comfort zone. Ow! I bumped my shin on a kneeler. It felt like it had when Chloe kicked me under the table. I was waiting in church for the organist, whom I was to meet at 11:00 AM.

The organist was by far the most serious musician at the abbey. I felt that Fr. Javier's piercing intellect knew exactly what I was doing from a socio/political, devotional/theological, emotional/aesthetic, historical/ontological, and psychodynamic/dramatalurgical point of view, but it was the organist who knew where we were going musically. I also had the sense that, since he understood the music, he intuitively understood all of that other rigmarole, too.

It was raining, and the organist's cowl was wet when he arrived; he must have cut across the courtyard. When we first met, he had freely admitted that he was a monk because he was a failure at life when measured along its typical metrics, and because he loved music. For him, *Rose Fire* was the most interesting thing that had come along in a long time.

Though he had not voiced this opinion explicitly — that the two of us were the only ones who knew what was *really* going on — he did take a conspiratorial attitude with me. I didn't know what was going on at all. But his conspiracy, with its winks and sly looks, was kind of infectious, so I went along with it.

He even glanced around occasionally, as if to see if anyone was listening in. He perceived clearly that neither the monks nor the students knew what *they* were really doing. By the end, I actually started to think that *I too* knew what was going on.

The organist favored a quick pace through the overture, so as to get Chloe on stage as soon as possible, before we lost the audience's attention, for it was her appearance that announced that this was serious shit (he said). By the way, he asked, how had I talked her into taking her clothes off? I laughed. "Her parents are nudists," I shrugged. "She said she's been running around naked all her life."

The penny whistle and the bagpipes would shatter the church, he said. The nude scene, the whistle, and the pipes were like poles holding up a circus tent, the sagging canvas being the attention of the audience, which he assumed was going to be on the verge of collapsing. He had a proposal: a fourth tent pole, so to speak. "What," he asked rhetorically, "holds the whole thing together? What binds the office, the rosary, and the AA meetings?" He looked around. "Isn't it none other than the presence of *you-know-who*?" he whispered, and he might even have winked.

His proposal was to add a leitmotif in the background when the presence of you-know-who was most intense. Since the play opened tomorrow (and closed tomorrow) and the dress rehearsal was yesterday, it seemed to me a little bit late to be modifying the score. But he was insistent. It would be like the production behind rock and roll, he pointed out. Personally, I like the tracks before they add the production.

"What did you have in mind?" I finally conceded, thinking of the overriding principle that held this all together, namely "What the hell?" He went to the organ and played a six-note leitmotif he had composed in such a high register that it sounded like angels on high announcing the presence of Christ.

"I will just salt them in at the appropriate junctures," he said, playing his riff in different variations for my approval.

He looked at me steadily. Then, without blinking, said, "I get it, you know."

‡

I had arranged to have lunch with the abbot in a private dining room deep in the internal recesses of the monastery; there were just the two of us. The abbot was an improbable-looking man with a grown out, natural tonsure of red and grey, with tufts sticking up around his ears. A white wine was served. The abbot asked about the monks on assignment with me, and about the organist ("a bit of a rogue, but one hell of a musician"). Had we come up with all the props? Were my actors all in good health? It was an easygoing conversation.

I told him about the rehearsal dinner and about the late addition of the leitmotif. We talked about the snowstorm and the revenant author of Matins. "A strange affair, altogether," the abbot allowed. I told him a little bit about my struggles with Lauds and hinted at my plans for Germany. Suddenly, as we were finishing our salads and about to start on the casserole, he changed directions. The white wine was taking its effect.

"You know, just because I am the abbot doesn't mean I am stupid," he said. "I know I am going to catch hell for the nudity. But what can they do to me?" punctuating his statement with a slice of eggplant on his fork. "The Bishop has no authority here; the Master General is in Rome. By the time they gather kindling for the fire, I'll already be pushing up daisies out behind the bell tower."

The thespian in him came out: "The nude scene is critical to the whole of the play. What if she appeared in a leotard? Then you would have exactly *nothing* on your hands." He paused, losing steam and apparently in great need of catching his breath. "By the way, how did you talk her into taking off her clothes?"

"Her parents are nudists, she said," I offered, echoing myself. "Running around naked all her life." How many people had I told this by now? How many people had believed it?

The abbot swirled the wine in his glass, then finished it off with a slight smack of his lips.

"No, I am honored to have this undertaking under my roof. Everyone thinks I am a buffoon. Well, everyone always thinks the abbot is either a buffoon or a tyrant, or has a mistress. This has always been so, and it will always be so. Thus, the lot of the abbot. This truly is a thankless job. I have been abbot twenty years and no one has ever said 'thank you.' Not once." He paused again to breathe. "I suppose I do drink too much wine."

Startled at this confidence, I took a deep swallow of wine myself.

"You know, Carl," the abbot said, throwing his arm around me and with a sparkle in his eye, "I kind of like this crazy caper. Let them think I am a buffoon! Of one thing I am certain: when the history of this monastery is written, several of the abbots will have their names misspelled!" At this he laughed until he coughed. He must have assumed that, as a Latinist, I would appreciate his remark.

After lunch, I wandered into the church. The pipe organ near the front was probably the largest non-agricultural purchase the monks had ever made. The altar was a huge black block of granite that had been shipped over by steam ferry from the other side of the Mississippi at a point in history when to order a block of rock to be delivered by steam ferry was simply matter-of-course. The ceiling was impossibly high. The rough-hewn stage, already in place for tomorrow, looked like a dreamscape. The giant hanging rosary notified all that something festive and out of the ordinary was about to go on.

Through the church windows, I could just see the tops of the iron crosses in the monks' graveyard. I wondered what it would be like to be buried there. I reflected that, as soon as the stage was rolled back out, and the giant rosary taken down, everything would revert to normal, as it had been forever. Or since 1848, at least. The monks who had been in the play would die and join the monks who had built the church and the monks who had first broken the sod with the plow, all of them together in the simple graveyard with the iron crosses.

I thought that, given time, there was a pretty good chance that no one at all would remember what was to transpire here tomorrow. Perhaps Chloe would tell her grandchildren about it some day. Perhaps the organist would tell some nephew or other, if one ever came to visit. It shouldn't take too long to die out completely.

But nothing is ever lost. We still receive light from galaxies that vanished aeons ago. So, too, I assured myself, our humble efforts tomorrow would spread out into the cosmos, whether there was anyone to hear us out there or not. I strongly suspected that there was someone listening. Otherwise, I would probably have stayed on at the Succulent Pig, perhaps picking up a degree at the New School, studying part-time and weekends, perhaps ending up myself teaching night classes in Political Theory, or American Art.

In hindsight, everything looks providential. It was certainly providential that Chloe's mother had, maybe even on a lark, arrived at that nudist camp for the first time, right? How else could this play ever happen? Looking back, it seemed to me like my whole life had been leading up to this. Was that trivial or profound? Taking a deep breath, I resolved to give it all I had—just as Chloe had promised she would do—or just as she surely would have, if given the chance.

I noticed on the way out of the church that there were some small stone chips on the floor along the edge of the walls. The walls were crumbling! They were 18 inches thick. How long would it take for the edifice to fall?

On our first meeting, the organist told me that once the monks had been eating in silence, as usual, when one of them jumped up and began to shout: "Nothing ever happens around this fucking place! Nothing ever happens around this fucking place!" Everyone continued eating in silence and eventually the errant monk also sat down and resumed eating in silence.

I left my reverie and set about what was laid out. First I called the chairwoman of the drama department. She had been doing everything she could behind the scenes to protect and promote the project: cajoling and organizing and stonewalling and whatnot. Somehow I had managed to leave her, that night at her condo, a secret sharer in a mystical adventure. She noted that we should serve bottled water at intermission. She said that Bob had already arranged to pick up the ice and had a couple of antique copper laundry tubs to put it all in.

"Perfect," I said. Who was Bob?

"We've been seeing each other," she answered my unasked question.

"I hope people show up," I said.

"Carl, believe me, it will be standing room only." Apparently she had been working on that aspect of things, too.

There was a long pause. I could not think of anything else to say.

"Well, alright, Carl," she said, and hung up.

Next I called St. Louis. When I floated the idea of going on to Germany to whomever it was that answered the office phone at Gethsemane Home, he said (and I quote): "Fine. Whatever." I don't think he actually knew who I was. I didn't know exactly who he was, either.

‡

Friday afternoon I went to attend to a family duty that I had been putting off: visiting Aunt Anne. She was not actually my aunt; rather she was the sort of once or twice removed older cousin one gets saddled with out of family obligation and the prior death of all more immediate relatives. Tradition had it that Aunt Anne had never missed Mass in her life. The truth, of course, was even more interesting: she had actually missed Mass only seven times, all of which she remembered clearly. She was delighted to see me.

"Carlito!" she pealed when I appeared at her screen door. "Come in! Sit down. What are you up to?"

For some reason it never occurred to me to ask her what she was up to. I just assumed that she had been living on and on in her little house, going to Mass every day and not doing much of anything else at all. I had expected her house to be full of religious kitsch, too, but this turned out not to be the case. It was just a regular little old lady's house, if not on the grand end of the spectrum of little old ladies' houses. Rosary beads, on an end table near her big chair, were the only clue that a bastion of the Roman Catholic Church lived here.

She scolded me for not visiting sooner. How had she known I was in town? But as I explained my project to her, she became very interested.

"I remember the snow," she nodded. "I ran out of coffee."

Her life was much the same, I supposed, day in and day out, waiting to die. Then, every once in a while, out of the blue, something would happen. Clearly, one such thing was my appearance and the news that the rosary would be performed the following evening at the abbey, and by Lutherans at that.

Still, she did not seem to be particularly surprised by my announcement of this, or my invitation to attend, as I proffered her complimentary tickets. Of course, she must go. She immediately excused herself to the kitchen and began to make phone calls (the phone was mounted on the kitchen wall) until she reached one Blanche, who was a decade younger and still able to drive at night, and who wasn't doing anything else tomorrow night anyway.

"Well, that's arranged," she returned and sat to face me. "Who do you think he *was*, Carl?"

"You mean the guy in the snowstorm?" I thought about that for a while. "Well, he certainly knew a lot about the rosary. He had read everything about the rosary, obviously, but he himself was hard to read. At first I thought he was unbalanced, but eventually I began to think it was something else."

I read my audience and added, "A fire burned in him. A revenant spirit, perhaps?"

"This *is* exciting," she clapped her hands together, then grasped mine. Her eyes were a hundred miles deep. I noticed that she still wore her wedding band.

"Do you think the Church can ever change, Carl? There was a visiting priest saying Mass last Sunday, some sort of missionary trying to raise money. At one point he actually said, pounding his fist, and I quote, 'We have got to get back to the past!' I did not give him even one dollar."

"To tell you the truth, I never give much thought to the Church," I sighed. Aunt Anne became very attentive all of a sudden, straining forward to hear exactly what I might say and squeezing my hand.

"I have thought mostly about ancient manuscripts. To me the Church is an oyster; I am interested in the pearl. But of course you can't have pearls without oysters." I looked nervously at my sleeve, which had been marred with white gravy the last time I had tried out this trope. "I suppose that the Church will be hurled into the future regardless of any strain to get back into the past."

She looked at me with her head tilted. "So, you just *dress* like a reactionary."

"Precisely," I replied.

"Well, then." She managed to get a lot of meaning into this throw-away phrase.

"Are you in the play?" she wanted to know.

"I read the lessons at Matins, wearing Domenicus's jacket." Version small.

She nodded.

We sat in near silence. Anne had an old pendulum clock that was nice to listen to.

"How did you talk Chloe into taking her clothes off?"

Anne finally asked.

I could not be absolutely positive, but I didn't think I had mentioned Chloe—and certainly not her nudity.

"Her parents are nudists. She has been running around naked all her life," I said in my, by now, well-worn explanation.

Anne raised an eyebrow skeptically. "I know her parents."

"I am going to Germany," I changed the subject. "Before he died, the author told me that Domenicus had written a *vita* under obedience. The monastery at St. Albans is gone, but its manuscripts are at the public library at Trier. They have the document. I thought I might have a look."

"Well, you would be able to read it," she pointed out unnecessarily.

Anne stood up and shuffled over to the end table to pick up her rosary. What was she, 95 by now?

"So, the beads are Jain, Christianity grafted on in 350, meditations added in 1415—by an alcoholic—and pictures added in 1483 by an unknown woodcut artist in Ulm," she mused, looking historically at her beads. "The woodcut artist may have been a woman."

Then she added, "Like a seed crystal dropped into a super-saturated solution, the pictures spread across Europe." Her movements might have betrayed her age, but her mind was certainly keeping up.

I broke in, "The author said he could never find anything definitively by the same hand in any of the books printed by any of the Gutenberg presses in Ulm."

"Had he been to Ulm? Maybe go to Ulm," Anne suggested. "See if you can find any ephemera that is not cataloged at the woodcut museum—posters, holy cards, calendars, playing cards," a slight pause here, but not quite as slight as I would have expected, given she was in the company of a man of the cloth, only loosely familial or not, "pornography, perhaps."

Her insight into the whole thing astounded me. She seemed quite conversant in matters I had never even heard of before except from a madman in a snowstorm. Had I *missed* something?

"When I talked to a clerk at Ulm, they said there was a box of stuff. Suppose I found, say, a playing card by the same hand?" I mused. "What more would I then know than I know now?"

"Not much, I suppose," Anne replied. "But you would know more than anyone else on this earth knows about the origin of the rosary."

I got up to leave.

"I will see you tomorrow night," she said. She insisted on seeing me to my car, and on the way out, she cut me a white rose from her garden.

That evening, I thought about calling Chloe. But what would I say, really? What hadn't already been said? I put Aunt Anne's rose in a glass of water. I went to Compline. Its haunting anthems rang in my mind as I sat in the dark church long after everyone else had gone to bed. I fished in my pocket for my key to the cloister: I had one more visit to make that night.

‡

I walked down the stairs from the church, let myself into the cloister, and headed down the long hall toward the blessed sacrament chapel. Everything was silent; almost everyone was asleep. Through the half windows, I could see into the courtyard: the shadowy fountain, the Gothic structure rising above, small desk lamps illuminating a stray handful of cell windows here and there. I walked slowly, leaning on the hickory cane I now carried sometimes at night. I bought it in the gift shop. It was perhaps some such scene as this that I envisioned my future would be like on the night of my conversion so many years ago.

No one was in the chapel. I sat on a wooden bench for a long, long time, thinking nothing. The lone candle in the sanctuary lamp licked and danced and sputtered, causing the shadow of the tabernacle to jump around the room. Then I rose and laid down prostrate in front of the tabernacle.

I laid there for a long, long time, too.

"God," I said at last, "I offer myself to you."

Silence.

I rose to my knees. I raised my arms in supplication. I felt the glossolalia forming deep in my being, then it burst forth in startling accents.

Then it was over. I had no sense of what the spirit had said, but the sense of having unburdened myself was strong.

Chapter XIX

Saturday morning I woke up early. I was glad I had brought my clubs up from St. Louis. I slipped into a polo shirt and chinos and headed for the links. I always feel silly dressed like that. But you simply do not show up at the first tee wearing a black suit and a Roman collar. In the first place, you will always get stuck keeping score. Then there is all this comical effort on the part of the other players not to cuss or say anything even slightly off-color.

When I arrived at the links, there were three IBM salesmen in the parking lot trying to put together a foursome; I fell in with them. A fourth IBM salesman had dropped out, apparently, because his dog was undergoing chemo and had spent all last night vomiting on the carpet. My IBM salesmen were all a little overweight and were also wearing polo shirts and chinos. I introduced myself as an adjunct professor teaching "over at Martin Luther."

They wanted to play for $10 a hole. I declined, for the simple reason that I am so good at golf, if I play for money, I am accused of being a hustler. So, I volunteered to keep score.

I teed off first, after which no one paid much attention to me, other than to roll their eyes in disbelief at my skill at the game. They talked about their houses and their mortgages and their yards and their kids and their wives and their bosses. They talked a fair amount about drinking and about "getting some," by which I gathered they meant chance, erotically-tinged encounters on the road that never really went anywhere. They asked me if I "got much," and I said that there "wasn't much" in paleography. What they talked about mostly was work. The air was blue with acronyms for software, mainframes, and contract clauses.

I encouraged them to call me "Shorty." As they got drunker, they did. "Hey, Shorty, give me a 7!" "Bullshit! Shorty, he shot 9," and so on. But it was a beautiful day for golf. My companions assured me that May was one of their top months in Iowa (along with October), but since they were all just passing through from Poughkeepsie or Raleigh or San Jose, what did they know about the local weather, really? Whatever. I loved playing among cornfields. One could even spot the occasional cow.

As luck would have it, the foursome behind us was comprised of "some." There were many furtive glances and much mis-estimation in my foursome of this group of what I can only call women around 40. We stayed at the clubhouse after the ninth hole for beers, so that group moved up and were then playing in front of us.

Why a foursome of women around 40 playing in front of us is so much more sexually stimulating than a foursome of women around 40 playing behind us, I could not say. Perhaps it was the extra beer at the ninth hole. In any case, my companions now became downright embarrassing, loudly revealing their social status and calling out "nice swing," and such like. If they heard, the women gave no indication and played on.

Then my companions got to talking about something called "The Cloud" (I could tell it should be capitalized by the reverent way in which referred to it), which they obviously didn't understand and to which they attributed fantastical powers—borrowed, no doubt, from marketing brochures. I saw a kind of parody at play between the erotic and the divine: the all-knowing Cloud above looking down at them lusting pathetically after the foursome in front.

On the twelfth hole, my drive passed one of the women, whose ball was deep in the rough where I could not see her; this is a minor infraction of golfing etiquette. When I came abreast of her, I tried to apologize for the boorish behavior of my companions, but she just laughed and said that it was the most attention they had gotten in a long time.

"Nice drive," she added. Then she stepped forth slightly to impart a secret — since I had been so nice, perhaps. There, on the twelfth fairway, the truth stood forth: all of these women were married to IBM salesmen themselves, just not to any of the IBM salesmen in my foursome. IBM must have a lot of salesmen.

Back at the clubhouse, as the boys waded into their sixth and seventh beers (but who's counting?), I added up the score. I shot a 67. The others allegedly had 92, 98, and 111, respectively.

"Shorty! You son-of-a-bitch!" That was the only feedback I got for what, I must admit, was a pretty good game.

"Gentlemen," I said, "I have had a wonderful time." I bought them all another round and excused myself.

I left them trying to sort out who owed whom what at $10 a hole.

‡

Back at the monastery, I had some time to kill. Chloe and I planned to get something to eat later, before the show, but that was at 5:00 PM; now it was only 1:00 PM. I grabbed my rosary and headed for church. The crude stage and

198

hanging rosary, and their impertinence, struck me again. Tomorrow, they would be gone.

The lumber from the stage would no doubt be repurposed; I could imagine some monk carefully prying out each nail and stacking the lumber as he dismantled the stage. The rosary would be disassembled, too, and the beads would revert to being Christmas tree balls, stored in large Styrofoam boxes in the basement of the university president's house, awaiting next December, when they would be hung once again on the big fir tree in the quad.

I was on the 13th mystery again, the descent of the Holy Spirit, my favorite. In my imagination, I had put Mary and the apostles up on the wooden stage. It was easy for me to imagine this scene: tongues of fire touching down on each of them—a picture I have seen a thousand times in medieval manuscripts. Next, I expanded the group. Domenicus emerges from drunken debauchery and adds fifty meditations to the beads, then turns his attention to alchemy and is buried by history. The woodcut artist in Ulm—a woman?—carves some rough pictures for a pamphlet supposedly to ward off the plague, then vanishes, perhaps carried off by the very same plague. I imagined them on stage, too: Domenicus and the woodcut artist. My mind wandered.

My desperate friend—how had he gotten to the monastery? I was headed for a dreary, more or less forced retirement. Then the snow. Then, like a cheap novel, a stranger dies, leaving behind a mysterious envelope and sending my life coursing in a new direction.

Sixty-seven. I had only shot a 67 three times in my life, and one glorious 66. Was it really credible that IBM salesmen did not recognize the wives of other IBM salesmen, just because they didn't happen to be *their* wives. And when did they start giving dogs chemo?

My erstwhile stranded-in-the-snow companion, Chloe, the abbot, the proctor, the organist, the chairwoman of the drama department, Bob (nice of him to bring water, the old copper washtubs, too—it would be a nice touch), Aunt Anne, Fr. Javier. I put them all up on stage. Our stage was not 7 feet in diameter; only in imagination would this mob fit on it. Touched by the fire. Then I imagined myself on stage with them. A flashing tongue of fire entered the chakra at the top of my skull.

I tend to be a man of realistic faith. I know that what God wants of me may not be much. I am unsurprised that forty years have passed since my original inspiration and its apparent fulfillment. I realize that the whole thing may go south if I am not attentive, and I know that being sufficiently attentive is beyond human capacity, as it necessitates true humility, which is also beyond human capacity. We all began to speak in other languages: Middle High German, Midwestern Lutheran Co-ed, Erudite Academic.

My wandering mind began to doze and come back, doze and come back.

"Hail, full of grace..."

I cleared the stage of all but Chloe. Chloe was naked. (Her parents were nudists.) She stood center stage, a single spotlight shining straight down on her.

She spoke: "I will tell you three things..."

"Hail, full of grace..."

"One: All is well."

"Hail, full of grace..."

"Two: What we do here reaches far beyond our galaxy."

"Hail, full of grace..."

"Three: All you need is love, love, love."

I wanted her to go on speaking. "Tell me three more

things," I nearly begged.

"You could not bear them," she replied.

She rose in all her glorious beauty and disappeared, up into the single spotlight. Although that happened in my imagination, I did not imagine it.

Two mighty thrones: on one sat Chloe, now in regal attire. The other throne was empty. I stood at the front of her throne, immaculately dressed, as usual. I was her steward. Ambassadors came, petitioners came, sycophants came. Each explained the details of their case to me. To each I assured in hushed tones, "Her parents were nudists. She has been running around naked all of her life." Then the proctor appeared.

"Wait! There has been a mistake! Her parents were not *nudists*. They were *Buddhists*," he nearly shouted.

"Jesus!" I said, regarding the large pile of affidavits, petitions, certifications, awards, proclamations, authentications, edicts, and appeals that would all have to be redone based on this new information.

Chloe descended from the throne and looked over the proctor's shoulder at the documents that he held.

"So my job is just ceremonial?" demanded Chloe.

"Anything but! Your job is eternal mother," I said.

"Doing without taking credit, that sort of thing?" asked Chloe.

"Exactly," I replied.

Domenicus wandered over. "Just how," he asked, "does one take a petition right to the queen without getting fobbed off on her steward here?"

Domenicus wandered off. I wandered off.

"My first proclamation as queen," said Chloe, I suppose to herself, "will be LOVE. L-O-V-E!"

"Lutherans!" I shouted back sardonically over my

shoulder.

At this point I must have fallen completely asleep. I startled awake as the monks began to file in for Vespers. I was late to pick up Chloe and headed straight for my car. I was to pick her up at her parents' house, not her dorm.

Chapter XX

I pulled slowly up Chloe's parents' long drive, climbed out of the car, and rang the door bell. Of course, they were all expecting me. Her mother answered the door.

"You're late," she said. The whole house smelled like cookies, and she was wearing an apron over her low-cut blouse; a rather foppish Easter bunny stared out at me from the front panel with large, jovial eyes. It occured to me that this slightly graying Midwestern woman before me did not quite seem to be particularly French, nor quite the type you would expect to have been frequenting a nudist camp in Basel in her youth.

"I fell asleep in church." A lame excuse.

The stepfather joined us, and I cleared my throat. Chloe had told me that her mother was Catholic, her stepfather a nominal Presbyterian. Lutheranism, which neither of them seemed to take very seriously, was a compromise. That seemed plausible, at least. Chloe's stepfather joined us. Deep in the house I heard *le petit* twerp holler "Chlo-eeeeeee! Your *father's* here!"

"Mom!" Chloe screamed.

Standing in the entryway, the stepfather asked about my golf game; he had apparently been on the links himself that morning.

"How did you do?" he asked.

"Not too bad."

"I heard you shot a 65," he persisted. News travels fast

in a small town.

"No, no," I laughed. "A 67. I have never shot a 65 in my life."

Chloe came downstairs dressed for the part: Jeans, a simple cotton blouse, the string of jasper beads, and the famous reticulated cowboy boots.

"Hello, *Father*," she called from the bottom of the deep-pile tan carpeted stairs.

"Carl was just telling me about his golf game," her stepfather said.

"I didn't know you played golf," Chloe accused, looking at me closely. She was actually mad.

"Where are you kids going?" her stepfather asked. I had to be older than him by at least a decade.

"Pizza at the Green Pepper," Chloe answered.

That was the first I'd heard of this; I thought our dinner plans were still indefinite.

"Well, we'll see you at the abbey." He looked like the kind of guy who would add "at 7:30 PM *sharp*," but he didn't. Instead, he stepped forward and gave Chloe a hug.

"Knock their eyes out," he whispered. He seemed nonplussed at the prospect of his daughter disrobing for a crowd, and it occurred to me that this would be the reaction of both a nudist stepfather *or* a stepfather who did not know that a nude scene was planned.

As we drove out of the cul-de-sac, we saw Marty driving by. Chloe waved, then rolled her eyes.

The restaurant was bustling. We sat in a booth way in the back, which suited me fine. The Green Pepper specialized in pizza baked à la wood oven. Chloe ordered spinach pizza with pesto and goat cheese.

"Sounds great," I lied. I would have preferred sausage and pepperoni.

On the table, there was a cheap plastic bud vase, and in the vase was a yellow rose. It must have been left in the booth by its previous occupants. Perhaps they were coming from a wedding? There were no flowers on the other tables. Chloe and I looked at each other.

"Why did you go to Martin Luther?" I broke the ice.

"Because I got in?" she shrugged. "I dunno."

Chloe was smiling sweetly and staring at the yellow rose. There was a matching piece of yellow ribbon tied to the vase.

"In the middle ages," I ventured, "the rose symbolized both mystical union with God and a woman's...," I searched for the right word. Chloe looked off behind me with a smile that I couldn't quite decode.

"Vulva," I landed on, for decorum, then regretted it. "That tension between mystical union and sexual union was all over the place and it runs through the heart of what we present tonight."

"You didn't mention that in class."

We waited for the pizza.

‡

Chloe wiped the grease off her fingers, there mostly from picking at her slice, not really eating it, and pulled her script out of her jeans pocket. It was well folded. Out next came an overly long and quite ostentatious rosary in filigreed gold and lapis lazuli. "What do you think Domenicus was like?" she asked.

"I suppose that he was rather a tortured soul," I offered.

"I met a guy at the bar last night," she said. "He was wearing this rosary around his neck. He might come tonight."

Great.

Neither of us were really hungry. Sizing this situation up, Chloe hollered to two boys a few tables away: "You guys want some pizza?"

"Sure!" They came right over *and joined us*, for Chrissake.

"What the hell is on it?" one asked.

Then, "What the hell is pesto?" But they tucked into it anyway, sliding into the booth, one on each side, after a brief struggle to see who would get to sit next to Chloe.

"How do you want me to undress before I climb the stage?" Chloe asked me casually, perfectly aware that she now had everyone's attention. The two boys had been chewing. They weren't anymore. She was good at this.

"However you undress in your bedroom," I said, buying into her gambit that we were just talking shop when some old friends just happened to drop by. "Do you fold your clothes neatly or throw them on the floor?"

"I throw them on the floor."

"Then throw them on the floor." I, of course, fold mine neatly.

"It's key to the whole thing, isn't it?" she asked, smiling slightly to herself. More weighty questions as the hour approached.

"Yes. Dispel the fog of churchiness, bring up the topic of real life, and ring the bell that reverberates throughout the work and into eternity."

"OK," she exhaled. "I am doing this."

"I have spent whole summers without a stitch on," she added, a bit uncertainly, in her French-ish accent.

I looked at my watch. Neither of the boys had resumed chewing yet. I wished they would leave, but I dared not rescind any invitation that Chloe had offered, even if accidentally. I continued to talk as if I was alone with her, changing the subject: "I am leaving early tomorrow morning for Germany."

"I'd hang on to those beads if I were you," I wanted to add but did not.

The boys finished the pizza, and Chloe promptly shoved one of them out of the booth. When I paid, I sent back a couple of pitchers of beer to wash it all down with, then went to wait in the car.

‡

I drove us slowly toward the monastery, taking the back roads. I think I wanted to minimize the time we had to just stand around and wait. Chloe looked radiant — we had definitely caught her on the right day.

"Don't worry," she said, nodding either to me or to herself or maybe both. "It's going to be alright."

In a way, how could it fail? The audience would surely be there mainly to see their kids, and there, sure enough, their kids would be. The monks would be given a curious memory with which to punctuate their otherwise ordinary existence. The inevitable inquiry was bound to go nowhere. The abbot would retire, perhaps to a sister abbey. The chairwoman and this Bob fellow would probably move in together. Or whatever. I was less sure of that. Chloe was touched by the fire, but if my reading of her was correct, she would invest this fire in an otherwise unremarkable life. With any luck, I would die in Germany, surrounded by nurses from the Philippines, perhaps, dragging out work on the critical English edition of *Liber Experimentarium* until I could see the finish line.

I glanced over at Chloe. She had been looking at me. "I

have the urge to sum up," I confessed.

"Forget it, professor."

There was something about the way she smelled. She stuck her head out the window and let the wind blow her hair into a wild tangle. When she pulled it back in, she looked just right for her part. Break a leg.

‡

When we arrived at the abbey, the parking lot was already jammed, and cars were parking along the road and on the grass. People were milling about, waiting until after Compline to enter the church. High in the tall pine trees, the crows were in an uproar, cawing until their little lungs were sure to burst. One frazzled crow was dashing from murder to murder as if it were trying to forge some weird crow consensus that enough was enough already.

Chaos reigned. One of the repertory actors had the stomach flu and could not act; her understudy was freaking out and bawling. Someone's uncle, who was supposed to bring the bagpipes, was seen entering a tavern with said bagpipes at 1:00 PM and was, as far as anyone could tell, still there. Someone was supposed to bring the programs directly from the printer; they had not yet arrived. Some of the penny-sized blue sequins had fallen off God's turban. One of the ushers was sewing them back on, but she had no thimble and kept sticking her finger. Some of the sequins were also now missing.

It also seemed someone had let the monastery cat into the church. The cat kept meowing, but nobody could locate it, let alone catch it, and now that the monks were singing Compline, they could not even search for it. And Marty, who had actually showed up, was acting weird. Amidst all the hubbub, Bob was calmly icing down bottles of drinking water in two magnificent antique copper laundry boilers. I liked his approach. Go Bob.

I gave instructions, comforted, encouraged. The box of spare blue sequins was actually in the glove compartment of my car, for some reason. We would pretend that the cat was part of the show, somehow. A squeal of bagpipes, as a newly arrived pickup lurched drunkenly off the drive and onto the lawn, signaled the end of that problem. The programs also arrived but were promptly dropped and were being blown all over the parking lot by the wind; a posse of cast and crew members was immediately formed to police them up.

Chloe's parents were standing on the grass with her brother, who was obviously attending under protest. Chloe said he had renounced their church and joined the evangelicals mainly, according to Chloe, to annoy his liberal parents. It is the genius of the second born to speak just loud enough to be annoying but not loud enough to have the parents come down too harshly on them. He had perfected saying "yeah, right" in this inspired register. He gave me the sneer that evangelicals seem to reserve just for priests.

Chloe's mother was possessed of considerable social skills; she took me aside and told me that Chloe was known to take some fanciful liberties, if I knew what she meant. I got the impression she might have talked to my aunt. "I don't know what gets into her sometimes," she laughed nervously. At least she could see that this was all kind of a hoot.

Compline over, the audience began to file into the church. Everyone's parents and grandparents were there. Jo Ann was actually there with her second husband; they must have found a sitter, because the child was nowhere to be seen. They seemed a little out of their element. Then there were a bunch of rowdy students: friends, roommates, everyone who had purchased a Monster Cookie for Carl. I think the only Catholics in the audience were a priest who happened to be staying over at the abbey, a woman who volunteered at the gift shop every third Sunday, and Aunt Anne. Marty was making faces at Chloe and scratching his crotch in a casual but persistent manner.

There wasn't enough room for everyone, so the abbot let the rowdy crowd into the cloister, and they became the groundlings, sitting on the floor by the stage. I liked that touch; Shakespeare, too, had had to deal with drunken groundlings. My students were carrying the props in on the long wooden benches. This gave the impression, I suppose, of experimental theater, but actually there was no other way to do it. Enthusiasm ran high.

The props were all in place. The audience quieted down. Then there was a curious lull. The abbot was missing. He, it turned out, was in the sacristy with Aunt Anne, whom it seemed he knew from somewhere way-back-when. The abbot and Anne were drinking a bottle of the monastery's finest 1903 and telegraphed "sorry" with his eyes when I finally found him in this tableau.

A fellow waiter of mine at the Succulent Pig used to say, "Every time I go on stage, I am prepared to die." Well, OK, then. I took a deep breath, and *Rose Fire* was set to begin.

Chapter XXI

The bell began to toll, the lights went out, Chloe's little brother said "yeah, right," just loudly enough to carry across the church. *Rose Fire* was underway. The organist coaxed masterful definition from his instrument. The audience didn't catch on at first that the opening of the show was taking place right in front of them, amongst the props. The first incident of the abbot's microphone being accidentally left on everyone took as an actual accident. Then the acoustics in that old stone church did something for the penny whistle that I never expect to hear again in this life. It was so pierce, it even quieted down the college students, and the attention the audience now gave to the stage was fierce.

When Chloe began to take off her clothes and throw them around on the floor and on the benches, it was as though she had gone mad. It was like watching a street person melt down on the subway. But when she mounted the stage naked (her brother gasped "Jesus!" as did her stepfather), it was clear: Eve, Mary. She had to give a little jump to catch the ladder — this started the stage rolling — someone had forgotten to lock the wheels. So when she stood on top in all her naked glory, the stage was actually rolling into the choir. A couple of stagehands quickly rolled it back to its place and then locked the wheels.

Some of the monks averted their glance; some looked.

I looked.

‡

The soaring chant swirled around our rustic stage and the drama unfolding on it. Even those monks I suspected of having serious reservations about the material began to give themselves to it. Actors touched the timing points like they were sacred, and the whole thing lumbered forward like a chain gang.

The disparate vignettes onstage reminded me of the cave paintings in the South of France: moving deeper into the cave, striking image after striking image looming, all seemingly unrelated, but at a deeper level so essentially related that the mind can barely grasp it. When Picasso first saw them, he remarked, "They knew everything."

When it was nearly time to read the first lesson, I looked at the faces in the audience: Chloe's mother lightly fanning herself with a program, her stepfather slowly chewing one side of his bottom lip, Aunt Anne somehow exuding that she was with me, the stunned groundlings wide-eyed amongst the tall—albeit Catholic—cotton. Did they seem to have the vague feeling they were watching something worthwhile? It was hard to tell.

Anyway, this was my moment. I donned the high-necked jacket and carried in the enormous book. I walked to the lectern like a bride approaching the altar at her wedding. I placed the book reverently on the stand, found my place, opened it slowly, and looked them all in the eye. Then I began: "We read."

Midway through Matins, there was a big commotion back in the sacristy—banging around, the thud of something large falling to the floor. The abbot went back to check, then returned with a big stage shrug to indicate that he hadn't found anything.

Then, during the reading of the seventh lesson, one of the actors got tangled up in the giant rosary somehow, and the whole thing came tumbling down, much to the delight of Chloe's brother. After a long, panicky pause, my students realized that nothing could be done except push it aside, with the intent of hanging it back up during intermission—the show must go on.

Then the cat jumped up on the organ keyboard and played a few random notes which the organist immediately turned into a little cat-leitmotif.

But the structure stood out as we had hoped: the three-threaded drama unfolding on stage, swimming in ethereal chant which, if anyone was listening to it, was a commentary on these very events. All of this punctuated by smudges of indelible humanity and raised to a curious level of reality by the Greek chorus.

So, in an obscure Trappist monastery, off a little-used blacktop road, miles from town, in the attendance of mostly Lutherans, the rose fire mouldered, then burst into clear rose flame. I did not care whether I lived or died, so honored was I to be there, and when I read at the lectern, I was completely open to whatever kind spirit would speak through me. And they arrived, one after the other, calling urgently, insistently, implacably:

"Take up your beads."

"Seek and you shall find."

And every time Chloe's brother shouted "yeah, right," I thought "yeah, right."

Chapter XXII

Just after the collect ("Hence it is clear that the rosary cannot be dismissed simply as a popular piety, but is rather an advanced tool for mystical union with God"), the doors were thrown open, the lights came on, and everyone — audience, actors, monks, even the cat, in that order — headed for the patio.

What a beautiful night. The crows were still fussing but had moved to the other side of the road. The actors were pumped. The monks, up way past their bedtime already, looked around with bleary eyes.

Two camps immediately materialized: parents and grandparents on the patio, where they began to gratefully discover Bob's impeccable water spread, and students and assorted hangers-on out in the lawn, where they felt more comfortable lighting up their smokes. The actors, too, after hugging their grandparents first, headed for the grass.

The monks caucused near the door, as if anxious to be let back in, except the organist, who joined the kids on the grass and lit himself up a Chesterfield King. Chloe was nowhere to be seen.

The monks, of course, were not aware that they were amongst Lutherans. If one lives in a monastery, one could easily forget that the Reformation had ever happened. The social skills of choir monks atrophy over the decades devoted to the office. Too, many men become choir monks because of limited social skills in the first place.

Nonetheless, they had been urged by the abbot to "mingle," and so they did remain outside. None took a bottled water. I'm not sure any of the monks had ever seen bottled water. The doughty grandparents were having their stereotypes of Catholics confirmed.

I decided to work the patio first, then head for the lawn. I grabbed a bottle of water. It was really cold. Fr. Javier approached.

"I didn't really think you were going to be able pull it off," he said.

I didn't know how to answer this, so I just smiled.

"I know, of course, how you did it," Javier continued.

"How?" I genuinely wanted to know.

"You dug a little deeper. I didn't think you had it in you."

"That's because Trappists think that all Jesuits live in their heads."

"That might not be too far from the truth," Javier conceded.

He was extending his hand; I didn't notice it at first because of the sleeve of his choir robe. When I did, I grabbed it gratefully. What a satisfying handshake: farmer, monk, prophet, saint. Someone yelled "Shorty!" I froze. My first thought was that someone from the Succulent Pig had re-emerged, a ghost from the distant past.

"Shorty!"

Looking around, I saw with relief that it was one of my golf partners from that morning. He made his way boisterously towards me, an attractive woman around 40 in tow.

"Shorty! I didn't know you were a priest." He introduced me to his wife, who took my hand.

"I heard about your 65," she said.

"67," I corrected.

"Shorty is a paleontologist," the man continued.

"Paleographer."

"Whatever. Plays one hell of a game of golf!"

His wife was still holding my hand. Did she have friends in the foursome that played in front of us? Her husband, a natural salesman, had already lost interest in me, since I was obviously not in the market for computer services, and had wandered away to work the crowd, leaving his wife with me. She realized she was still holding my hand and let it go with embarrassment, or a tinge of regret. She looked at me sharply.

"Where did you learn to play golf?" she asked a little suspiciously, or possibly flirtatiously.

"I was on the golf team in high school," I lied.

It turned out that she was the mother of Chloe's understudy who, not called upon to act, was having the time of her life ushering, managing props, and generally cheerleading the cast. Her mother said it was good that Chloe didn't get sick, because her daughter wouldn't even let her see her naked anymore, ever, let alone a whole church full of people.

"Chloe's parents are nudists," I pointed out.

"Right, of course," the woman nodded. Slowly, her brows knitted. "Well, I'm glad she didn't get sick." She continued to look at me with sharp interest and narrowed eyes: there was something she wanted to know but could not ask — perhaps because she herself did not know what it was? I felt a distinct desire to satisfy her curiosity. Of course, the audience knew nothing of the reactionary bishop that ran me out of Chicago, or the tortured soul who handed me the script on the day of the night he died.

I asked her with my eyes: "Is there something you

would like to ask me?"

She shook her head slightly. Perhaps it was something like: What-is-it-like-to-be-a-priest-how-does-one-become-Catholic-where-can-I-get-some-of-those-beads-are-you-in-love-with-Chloe-I-thirst-and-what-is-the-meaning-of-life-anyway? I realized that my hands were back in hers. Then she spotted the water.

"Ah, water," she said, and moved away toward it.

I wandered around, doing a little eavesdropping. Corn, it seemed, had closed at $7.01 Friday. The river was at 14.2 feet and rising. Rain was expected again on Monday. There was some tsk-tsking about the nudity and a fair amount of which-one-is-yours-ing regarding the cast in general. Someone allowed that the chant was "eerily beautiful." Most of the people seemed to know each other already. They realized that they were in the avant-garde, theater-wise, and were trying, though largely failing, it seemed, to rise to the occasion. The phrases "post-Modern," "Chautauqua," and "paradigm shift," having made their way inland over the decades, now wafted through the lovely evening air on the prairie. When the crows took a break from their fussing, I could hear the not-quite-organic cattle lowing on the hill across the road.

"Carl! Oh, Carl!" The chairwoman of the drama department knifed her way through the crowd with Bob in tow. I thanked Bob for the water and indicated that I was about to enjoy one.

They had emerged from the church with the abbot and Aunt Anne; clearly they had finished off the '03 after Matins, and I suspected that Chloe had joined them.

"I think it must be understood as folk art," I said ironically.

This remark registered with her immediately, and I

could tell that she could not wait to get away and pass this insight on to others. She didn't catch the irony, possibly because of the wine. Bob, who was drinking only his own water, would surely not have noticed irony under any circumstances and looked rather relieved to have been so enlightened, by the director, no less. I had the urge to rush to the other side of the patio and see how long it took the "folk art" rumor to get over there.

My dear mother used to say, "It wouldn't kill you to be nicer once in a while." This is true. If it were not for the chairwoman, I would never have been able to carry this caper off. I began to regret my supercilious remark. On the other hand, there seemed no point in now trying to convince them that it wasn't folk art. Whatever. I took both of their hands.

"I'm not as dumb as you think I am," the chairwoman said. This caught both me and Bob off guard.

"Listen," she let go of my hand and got right in my face. "Closely."

She actually was poking me with her finger. "I. Was. Glad. To. Help. Got that?"

Bob moved a little closer to her, to protect his turf.

"Are you going to the after party?" she asked, removed once again to a safe distance, her index finger curled harmlessly back around her water bottle.

They mingled left, while I mingled right. I could hear her: "This is best understood as folk art," she was explaining to some of the more horrified-looking parents.

"Hey, Preach!" I have observed before that a Roman collar means something different to Lutherans than it does to Catholics.

"Have you ever seen that sentimental slop on TV where some old battle ax nun leads the rosary in a fake-devout voice with schmaltzy music in the background, concluding with about a yard and a half of Catholic boiler plate?" This was Jay's father. He smelled a tad drunk, and I think that seeing Chloe naked had put him in a reckless mood. "What the hell's the deal with that?"

I liked this guy.

"In medieval China, people wore their prayer beads," I replied. "Richer people had more expensive beads, of course. At court, what your beads were made of hinted at your rank. Eventually, the beads just became an insignia of rank, people having ceased praying on them centuries before."

"You're OK, Preach," he said, grabbing my shoulder. "I heard about your 71."

"67," I protested. I was beginning to get a handle on small town life. Since he didn't leave, I offered, "I hear corn closed at $7.01."

He looked me right in the eye. "I am not stupid, Preach," he said, drifting away.

I mingled right and found myself talking to one of the monks. "This is the most exciting thing to happen around here since the old round barn burned down," he said.

I thought it was a joke for a minute, but he continued, "I was just a novice. The volunteer fire departments from all the little towns came, but there was nothing they could do. I heard about your 67."

"You're the first person to get my score right."

"I added 2 to one rumor and subtracted 3 from another," he explained matter-of-factly.

The monks all dress alike, but I knew this one was a priest because I had seen him vested for mass. Aside from our sacred duties at the altar, this priest and I could not have been more different. He was a farmer, I was a high-powered intellectual (at least that's what they called me in the *Chicago Tribune* once).

"I like the work," he said. "I am anxious to see how Act II goes down."

"You and me both."

"*The Romance of the Rose* had two authors—the first one died before the work was finished," he continued.

"That's right!" I had completely forgotten this detail.

"You have tradition on your side."

"Exactly!"

"You seem like a nice guy," he said.

I nodded, probably a little too enthusiastically.

The abbot grabbed my sleeve. He looked at me drunkenly as if I were the fulfillment of prophecy: "Now, thanks to you, something has actually happened around here!"

He leaned in with a conspiratorial air. "You know, that is the first time in my life I have ever seen a woman naked. Beautiful," he cough-laughed. "Anyway, thanks, man."

Then he held out an old, oddly shaped gold ingot. "The brothers buried these during the Civil War. We found them when the round barn burned. I give one away occasionally. I'd like you to have one." I extended my hand, which sank immediately under the weight of the gold. He drifted away and I found myself talking to Chloe's parents.

"The abbot-yay seems a little bit unk-dray," her mother allowed. She had the same look on her face as the IBM salesman's wife. I felt the need to defend the abbot, holding, as I was, his gold in my hand.

"He is under a lot of stress," I offered. "It's a thankless job." I showed them the gold ingot. Underneath an embroidered bolero jacket, Chloe's mother was wearing a tight-fitting dress from which her bosom should have been about to explode but somehow wasn't. When she took the gold bar, not expecting it to be so heavy, she dropped it, then immediately stooped to pick it up. Chloe's stepfather seemed immensely entertained by the whole thing. He took the gold bar and appraised it carefully.

"I'll give you $100 for it," he said.

"Add a zero."

"It's worth more than that," he laughed, weighing it in the scale of his hand.

After an awkward moment of silence, Chloe's mother turned to her husband: "You're *always* summing up," she laughed. "Sum up!"

"Well...," he said, giving himself time to think.

"You must come to the after party," her mother said to me in the meantime.

Chloe's stepfather cleared his throat. He was going to sum up!

"Something happened here tonight...," he trailed off. "Chloe...," he started again, then stopped in the manner of a man used to summing up much more effectually than this. He cleared his throat. "As I was saying, Chloe has had an unbelievable experience to cherish the rest of her life."

Her mother looked at me. I think women must think that men will just automatically know what their meaningful glances mean. It was a holy moment nonetheless: all three of us, standing there, speechless.

Then the crows broke out in raucous cawing again; Chloe's parents mingled right and I mingled left. There, dead in my tracks, was Chloe's little brother. Twerp. I had had the vague idea of trying to win him over with my subtle charm, so he wouldn't be such a pain in the ass during the second act.

"I gather you subscribe to a metaphysic that is at

variance with this evening's proceedings," I said.

"Hogwash!" he spat out.

I had heard this expression all of my life but now began to wonder whether, in this agrarian setting, it it had some literal meaning that I had overlooked.

"Bullcrap," followed.

This term seemed to allow for less ambiguity.

"OK. What'll it take to shut you up?"

"Fat chance."

He had spoken only four words but was managing, nonetheless, to convey quite a lot of information.

"A man of few words," I ventured.

"No," he snorted. Then, "I am United Brethren," fire and smoke coming from his nostrils, almost.

"Ah." I could not remember, for the life of me, what the United Brethren are supposed to believe in. "They don't use prayer beads?" I ventured.

"They do not believe in superstitious rubbish," he shouted. This was more than he had had to say heretofore altogether. I should have written this guy into the script.

"Well, I should hope not!" I said.

Now I couldn't figure out how to get rid of him. He had no experience mingling on patios, otherwise he would have taken a natural nod and duck to the left, and I could have ducked right at the next opportunity... but for now we were stuck with each other. I thought of several other things I could say: "How about school this term?" "Praise Jesus!" "Be nice to your sister." How many times had he probably heard that? "Your mom is really stacked." "Nice evening." Deciding to cut my losses, I selected the last one.

"Nice evening."

"Popery!" was his final sally. I don't know. He seemed like a nice kid. It is hard to have a beautiful older sister, I suppose.

On the far side of the patio, I saw someone who looked familiar, so I used this as an excuse to slip away. I made my way over there, but by the time I got there, he was gone. But there was Aunt Anne. She looked magnificent; I could have mistaken her for Spanish royalty. She was a little bit drunk. She had a rosary wound around her left hand, an expensive one of silver and garnets. She was exuberant.

"I dearly loved my rosary, Carlito," she said, "but I feel like you have set it free."

Clearly Anne thought that the significance of the evening was that the Church, at long last, was ready to change. It was pretty clear to me that this little aberration in the back woods wasn't going to change the Church. Much like the proverbial gull that picks up a silk scarf and brushes the Rock of Gibraltar, it will be a long time before Gibraltar falls. At most, this evening would result in not just one but three abortive inquiries: diocesan, Trappist, and Jesuit. The thought of three abortive inquiries amused me.

But looking into Anne's lovely eyes, which were a million miles deep, I thought, why not? A frontal assault on Rome was bound to fail, but perhaps guerrilla war, starting obscurely in the provinces...

"Ah, Carlito, Chloe really is lovely," Anne remarked, apropos of nothing in particular. "You still headed for Germany?"

"Early tomorrow."

"What do you really expect to find there?"

"I expect I'll find that Domenicus was indeed an alcoholic. I'll go to Ulm to see if I can find a playing card."

"What will you know if you find one?"

We had been over this. Old people!

"Not much." Once more I looked into those eyes. "Do

you love her?" her eyes asked. But all she said was, "Auf wiedersehen."

"Auf wiedersehen," I replied.

Unlike Chloe's brother, Anne knew how to mingle: she mingled left as if she had mingled with bishops and kings, putting a copper tub of drinking water between us, while I mingled right, ducking down the steps to the grass.

Chapter XXIII

Chloe had already made her appearance, unnoticed by me.

"How'd I do?" she asked. She was jumping up and down a little bit.

"Magnificent!" I said. The young, I knew, crave approval, and I heaped on as much as I dared. I told Jay his Job was "abject." I told Cassie her God was "definitive."

"We are all going to my house afterwards. Please come! Brother Organist is coming, aren't you, Bro. O?" Chloe cooed at me, and then at him. Bro. O gave a little ready-to-party dance.

Chloe had drawn near and taken my arm; she could not stand still. She began blowing in my ear, not like a lover, but like one blowing smoke (which she was).

"I can't stay long," I apologized in advance.

"Yes!" She began jumping up and down again, and clapping her hands.

"Where did Marty go?" I asked, looking around.

"He freaked and split," someone said. Just as well. It was almost time to start again.

"Listen," I said. "Our fiery and alcoholic friend got the history of the rosary right. And he knew that the power to stabilize the mind and evoke God is in the beads themselves."

The kids, being young, naturally sided with authenticity, idealism, and passion.

"Look, the question is, can the fire that burned in his heart also burn on the earth, or is it destined to be snuffed out by the wars, by the Church, by the greed that has gotten loose in the land?" I surprised even myself at the passion I put into this little speech.

In any case, we headed back for the church like a high school football team running back on the field after halftime, the score with the cross-town rival tied at 7-7. Chloe was still jumping up and down, then kissing me on the cheek, then hugging me, then she lifted me off the ground from behind. It occurred to me that she, too, might be a little unk-dray. They say that the 1903 is a great vintage.

It was at this point that Marty reappeared, coming in from the woods across the drive, yelling, "Jesus Christ! Motherfucker! Son-of-a-bitch! Goddamn!" It went downhill from there. What about him? he wanted to know. What about his part? Why was no one hugging and kissing him? For, indeed, the hugging and kissing had sort of spread to the rest of the cast. Everyone was so startled that no one knew what to say.

Somewhere along the line, these good Lutheran youths had been taught to be compassionate. But, of course, their compassion only made his rage burn hotter.

"The rosary is a bunch of crap!" He grabbed a string of beads from one of the actors and flung it into the night. "Catholicism is a bunch of superstitious crap! I piss on it!"

Here he unzipped his pants and began to urinate in the direction of the abbey. The prevailing winds, however, worked against him; the piss on his hands and on his pants only enraged him further.

"Whore!" he screamed, moving toward Chloe and spitting repeatedly. "Whore!"

Chloe backed away slowly. I had never performed an

exorcism; as I have attempted to make clear, I am an academic. But, I figured, there is a first time for everything, and no one else had the presence of mind to do anything.

I slipped in front of Marty, pointed to the horizon, and commanded "Get Thee Hence," using the King James translation, since he was a Lutheran. This startled him, and he stopped advancing. He looked around in terror at what he had done, then lit out like a rabbit: he ran down the drive, across the road, and into the fields, screaming wildly. I reflected that, since we were in rural Iowa, he would be in no particular danger.

One of the girls asked, "Should we go after him?"

"Unless a cow sits on him, he should be alright," I said. This attempt at levity fell flat.

Chloe was sobbing, "I can't go back in. I can't go back in."

"Listen," I said. Everyone gathered round. Chloe settled into an occasional sob, punctuated with deep hiccupping sighs. The organist moved to my side and quieted people down with soft gestures. "What we are doing here tonight is real."

"What do you mean 'real'?" someone asked.

Pre-law moved to my side; he wore thick black-framed glasses and was a philosophy double major. "Look, we are not characters in a novel. We are actual people. We are going to college at Martin Luther. We are running from a reactionary bishop. We are seeking union with God," he gave a nod to the organist.

"Point, Charles?" asked Chloe, moving closer to him. Charles!

"The point is, it looks like what we are doing has been scripted, but who is writing the script?" he confirmed.

He had no real interest in acting, or the theater, and was

just trying to get his grade point up, so that he could get into law school. He was more than happy to usher and manage props and collect his A.

"You go along, you live your life, you never get the feeling it is scripted," he continued. "But then, all of a sudden, you are caught up in a pattern that seems realer-than-usual, like something is going on." (Not to self: Make than an A+.)

I could see that Chloe was straining to assimilate all of this.

"Look. Marty is just Marty. We all know that. He's probably in love with you," he said to Chloe. She shrugged.

"He had probably never seen a girl naked before," pointed out the organist. "Neither had I."

Some people laughed.

"Didn't you ever have a little boy push you down because he liked you?" I asked. That seemed to register. People were beginning to file back in, oblivious to the little drama on the grass. Chloe saw her mom and stepdad and the twerp filing back in.

Chloe looked at me. "Fucker," she said. But it didn't matter. The show would go on.

So, cigarette out, taking a deep breath, Chloe headed back in. We all headed back in.

Chapter XXIV

The organist was visibly pleased to be involved in "happening stuff." He took Chloe's arm on the way back into church and began discussing the musical backdrop of one of the vignettes with her. She nodded as he spoke.

The crows were fussing farther off now. Just the act of physical movement began to dispel the sour mood that Marty had cast. The actors were once again concerned with remembering their cues and the synchronization points with the choir. They began making sure props were in place for the quick scene changes of Act II. When Chloe and the organist passed by me, Chloe squeezed my arm a little too hard. Back on the patio Bob was happily collecting half-empty water bottles; the ice water had been a huge success.

The monks were arranging their music. The lights went out and then began to come back on slowly, as is called for in Lauds. The choir began to chant the first antiphon, and Chloe, fully clothed, mounted the stage for the first vignette of the first glorious mystery — the resurrection. Immediately the apostrophe which opens Lauds began, and Chloe stood on the stage alone and watched the Greek chorus split apart.

In a sort of reverie, I began to reflect on this curious material.

‡

> *When the wicked heresy of the Albigensians was growing in the district of Toulouse... St. Dominic, who had just laid the foundations of the Order of Preachers, threw himself whole-heartedly into the task of destroying this heresy.*

As far as I know, this was all basically true. But then:

> *As everyone knows, she instructed Dominic to preach the rosary to the people as a unique safeguard against heresy and vice. St. Dominic began to promulgate and promote this pious method of praying.*

This is pure hooey. There is not a shred of truth in it.

> *And the fact that he was its founder and originator has been from time to time stated in papal encyclicals.*

This is certainly true. Countless papal encyclicals—more than a hundred—solemnly repeat this pious nonsense.

> *All to the contrary... Is ANATHEMA!*

As if shouting anathema would make the truth go away.

‡

Anathema still seemed to be reverberating off the walls, when I heard the muffled crack of a rifle and glass shattering in the back of the church.

My first thought was that, the truth about the rosary being out, the counterattack had begun. Then, coming to my senses, I realized that, closer to home, somebody was actually shooting at us. A second shot must have entered through the broken window — an intricate Gothic shape way up high, near the rafters. It ricocheted around off the stones inside the church; this was dangerous.

A kind of controlled panic broke out. The men in the audience got all the children and some of the slimmer women under the pews, which were made of solid oak. The chaos had a strange effect on the monks; they began milling around as if Mass had ended early and the coffee wasn't quite brewed yet. The organist brought up the house lights, which made everything seem a little less crazy.

I ran to the door of the church and looked out. In the pool of gold cast by the yard light high above the scene, I saw Marty in the parking lot with what appeared to be an old Winchester Model 94 raised to his shoulder. When I yelled "Marty, drop it," some people were able to figure out what was going on.

Suddenly, two of my props managers charged around me at full speed. They stormed the parking lot and knocked Marty to the blacktop, wrestling the rifle away from him and breaking his trigger finger. They then proceeded to sit menacingly on him until reinforcements should arrive.

My students!

The reinforcements did soon arrive. Well, as soon as was to be expected. Somebody had a cell phone, and fifteen minutes later, two sheriff's cars squealed up the drive, lights strobing and sirens wailing.

After the deputies had taken over with Marty, people began to come out of the church and onto the lawn, trying to piece together what was happening, then passing their partial knowledge on to those behind them who knew even less. There were still a few bottles of water in the copper laundry tubs, and a couple of people helped themselves.

Men were standing so as to protect the women, in case there was any more trouble.

By now one of the deputies was leading Marty— handcuffed, bloodied, sobbing—to a patrol car. The other deputy was talking to the abbot, whom he seemed to know. One had the sense that things were wrapping up, even though things had only started going haywire less than 45 minutes ago. Chloe had joined her parents. My two student heroes of the night were being congratulated all around.

I had the curious sense that the long arc of my faith, kindled in a smoky jazz club in the West Village, and hardened like steel among the dying in the rice paddies of Vietnam oh so many years ago, had come back to Earth here, amidst the blue strobe lights atop the sheriff's cars, the murder of crows screaming in the pine trees overhead, and the herd of spooked Black Angus shifting and snorting and pressing against the fence across the road.

Some of the monks just went off to bed. Everyone else was now outside waiting for someone to tell them what to do. That someone was, inevitably, me. Chloe came over, tears streaming down her face. The abbot was looking at his watch. I raised my hand, and everyone quieted down.

"I want to thank you all for coming. Under the circumstances, I think we had better call it a night." The show would not go on. I was never going to see my version of Lauds performed. I would probably survive.

There was general agreement, and people began to move quietly toward their cars. Chloe's stepfather yelled after them, encouraging everyone to come over to their place anyway—the after party would go on, even if the show did not.

"Are you coming over, Father?" he asked. He had never called me father before, had he?

"You could come for just a little while," Chloe's mother said, indicating the shaken Chloe with a nod.

"For a little while," I promised.

Almost everyone was gone. Bob was pouring ice on the grass. Javier was still there. "You should have written that into the script," he cackled. "*Shots rang out!*"

"I think someone may have written it into the script," I quipped. "But it wasn't me."

It seemed like he accepted this as explanation. To Javier, that might seem perfectly reasonable. He had been in this same place—singing the same psalms—since shortly after the war. Slight changes in the routine were quite noticeable to him and tended to have meaning.

"Is the boy alright?"

"The sheriff took him."

He looked up at the shattered window. "That won't be any problem," he nodded.

Chapter XXV

Chloe's parents had quite a bash planned and were now circulating among the high-tailing-it guests, actively encouraging them to come over. As the story of what had *actually* happened moved through the crowd—almost everyone had had to deal with Marty being Marty at one time or another, it seemed—the idea of a party wasn't anywhere near unthinkable. So, most of them showed up.

The party was in two tiers: keg beer in the basement for the underage drinkers (there was also a local band playing) and the great room upstairs for the adults, where there was a bar with a bartender set up. A gypsy cab was parked prominently in the driveway, engine running, driver behind the wheel. The twerp was staying over with a friend.

Chloe's parents lived on this cul-de-sac because they were well-to-do. Seth's parents lived on the same cul-de-sac because they needed a big house for all of their kids; they might also have been well-to-do.

Seth's entire family was in the great room. His brothers and sisters had not been at the play but had run over barefoot across the lawn for the party. The bartender had found them some pop somewhere and they were all tearing about. Everyone was telling Seth what a great job he had done; he was really pumped up with all the attention.

Seth's parents, too, were accepting congratulations (and drinking pop). They liked the apocalyptic ending, which they took to be part of the play, although his mother thought it was a little bit too realistic; she had been hit with some shards of glass but was not harmed. They didn't stay long.

At the door, Seth's mother said it was refreshing to meet a priest who took the literal sense of scripture seriously. I took that as a compliment.

"Praise the Lord," I said, as she shoved her little army of kids through the front door. I noticed that the van in their driveway had a bumper sticker: "In case of Rapture, this vehicle will be abandoned." I saw a bumper sticker once that said: "Being nice to people is a really good idea." Unitarians, probably.

Chloe's parents were wonderful hosts, though they both seemed to be avoiding me. Her stepfather stood in the middle of things and beamed, while her mother moved graciously around introducing people who didn't know each other, making sure people got a drink, and the like. The plan was, they would stay until all the adults left, then they were going to spend the night at a bed and breakfast across the river. Chloe's friends were welcome to stay over, take the gypsy cab home, or whatever.

The chairwoman of the drama department showed up wearing my yellow Cat-in-the-Hat hat, with Bob on her arm. This sparked a round of applause in the great room.

Chloe made a grand entrance carrying a dozen red roses and wearing a tight-fitting red evening gown, surely borrowed from her mother's closet. She, too, was beaming. She had clearly gotten over it.

Blue jeans mixed easily with evening dress. I knew it was the last time I would ever see Chloe. Under such circumstances, one must choose one's words carefully.

"You are beautiful," I told her.

"Thank you."

Chloe was now Queen of the May. She took some of her

long-stemmed roses and cleverly wove them into a wreath, which she perched atop her head. Parents were beginning to leave. Marijuana smoke was drifting in from the patio. The band was getting going in the basement.

They say that a quarterback has a clock in the back of his head that counts down how long before he is going to get sacked. We Jesuits also have a clock in the back of our heads that counts down how long at a social event that includes both Protestants and alcohol it will be until we get sacked. I calculated that I had twenty minutes. I took Chloe's hand, and we headed for the basement. There was a computer-generated banner over the makeshift bandstand which read "It Happened Once at a Monastery Near Dubuque." Chloe began to dance by herself in front of the bandstand.

I was dressed, as usual, in an impeccable black suit with a Roman collar. I began to sway to the music and move across the floor toward her. The band amped up. We took each other's hands and began to move in some ancient, unknown way. When the band took a break, I said I needed some fresh air and headed out the French doors to the patio. Outside was all guys.

"Where'd you learn to dance like that?" one asked.

"She was leading," I shrugged.

When the band started up again, I saw that Chloe had found another partner. Her shoes were off. It is easy to slip away from people who are smoking dope. When they looked up at a low-flying helicopter ("Hey, man!"), I ducked through a hedge.

Back at the monastery, someone had already put cardboard over the broken window. I walked along the lonely cloister, then down into the adoration chapel: some benches, a candle, the tabernacle. I lay before the tabernacle on the cool stone floor. A long time passed. Suddenly I was aware that I had vanished and had now reappeared. In that absent moment, I understood my life, my priesthood, *Rose Fire*, and my ever-impending death.

I had one more thing to attend to back in my room. I took out my final grade report ledger, which the college still allowed older faculty to use in lieu of the new computer system. I would mail it in the morning. I checked the box "correction." Then I printed carefully:

MARTY LANGSTON.
FINAL GRADE: INCOMPLETE
AMENDED TO: A

Chapter XXVI

I didn't know how long it would take to get through security, so I arose at 4:00 AM the next morning, which was Sunday, and had one of the brothers drive me over to the airport, which was nearby. He was driving my old car, the title for which I had signed over to the abbot only yesterday. The brother who drove had nothing to say; involved mainly with the farm, he knew little of the events which had recently transpired, aside from that I was involved in them and that someone shot out a window in the church.

When we got to the airport, it was closed. It was the smallest airport I had ever seen. So much for arriving two hours early. I told the brother not to wait, I would be fine, there was a bench. I sat in the dark. There was a little breeze. Finally, headlights loomed up and a van pulled into the parking lot. The van had a bumper sticker: "Need a weapon? Pray the rosary!" What the hell is that supposed to mean? It was the airport manager.

"Sorry, Father," he said. "We don't have many on the early flight on Sundays, Father. Is there anything I can get you, Father?" In short, the kind of Catholic that drives me crazy.

There were eleven of us flying to Chicago. When security arrived, she cleared us all in seven minutes. With a little profiling, I reflected, she could have cut it down even more. My companions were all soybean farmers. They were headed for a soybean conference in Chicago and would also tour the Board of Trade.

When we took off, I tried to make out Chloe's house, which was in a subdivision on the same side of town as the airport. Maybe I saw her cul-de-sac, maybe not; there were so many of such similar ilk, so I could not be sure.

When I got to O'Hare, my flight to Berlin had been canceled because of terrorist threats. However, I was able to change my ticket to Brussels by way of Iceland. From there, I could take the train.

The work before me was not daunting: *Liber Experimentarium* was written in the 15th century. The manuscript was there. I had a carrell reserved at the Stadtbibliotech Trier, where I could work; I had talked to the clerk already. There was at Ulm a museum devoted to 15th century woodcuts. They had several boxes of ephemera which had not been cataloged; it was not impossible that I would find a match.

I tried to pray my rosary on the flight to Iceland from Chicago, but I drifted in and out of slumber instead. My thoughts were confused. I saw Marty leading a vast, raging mob. Chloe's naked beauty was driving them to fury. She turned around, then bent over and touched her toes to feed their insane distraction. A swing on yellow ropes was lowered—it looked like a Las Vegas show. Chloe stood on the swing, held one rope in her hand, and was lifted into the heavens just before the mob stoned her. I woke up. *Hail, full of grace...* Then I dropped off again.

I saw Chloe in a pool of her own blood, dead, on a futon, wearing only panties. Two men were standing over her in broad brimmed fedoras: detectives. The chief of detectives arrived. He, too, wore a broad brimmed fedora:

"What have we got here?"

I woke up. *Hail, full of grace...* I drifted off.

I was in a firefight in Vietnam. Young men all around were dying. Some were calling on Jesus, some were calling for their mothers—Chloe was a nurse, working at my side. She worked fast, to determine if there were any who could be saved. There was a single shot; she dropped, her heart blown completely away. I took her hand and began to mumble the words of absolution.

I woke up. *Hail, full of grace...* I drifted off.

God, my judge, was sitting behind a small table. He was wearing the slightly comical turban covered with large blue sequins. He was looking over my file, just a few sheets of paper. It seemed to me that my file should have been bigger. Then He looked at me.

"You probably don't remember," he said, "but you served me a Po' Boy once."

It seemed to me that I did remember serving him once, at the Succulent Pig.

"I liked the play," he chuckled.

God wrote a hasty note on my file, then handed it back to me.

I awoke and looked out the window. The plane had begun its final descent into Reykjavik. Almost there.

FINIS.

EXCURSUS

Upstate New York
St. Irenaeus

Rose Fire was next performed at the distinguished Catholic boarding high school in upstate New York, St. Irenaeus. Small and expensive, it caters largely to the problem children of very wealthy New York City residents. Silvia Cronin, a new coach assigned to Drama Therapy, had just graduated from the New School and was determined to mix things up a bit. She stumbled across news of the play while looking for something else on the Internet.

It was an elaborate production in collaboration with the Music Therapy department; the school auditorium was fitted out to look like a neo-Gothic monastery for Parents Night. St. Irenaeus had so much money that the small round stage they ordered came out looking like a piece of fine cabinetry. Ms. Cronin had it destroyed and a new stage made of old packing crates.

Ms. Cronin had also enlisted her students into a conspiracy of silence during rehearsals. When, the night of the play, the prom queen (and daughter of a prominent hedge fund manager) appeared on stage naked, pandemonium broke out.

The actress's family was a major benefactor of St. Irenaeus; some have suggested, uncharitably, that she never would have been admitted otherwise. In any case, suffice it to say, they were not nudists (or even Catholic, for that matter). The later repercussions were endless: The Bishop, the Board of Governors, the alumni association, you know how it goes. But, of course, at that level of society it is understood that the show must go on, and go on it went.

There was a shortage of boys in Music Therapy, so many of the monks were actually played by girls. The abbot was played as an outsized fop, and all of the Greek chorus was rewritten and presented as rap. The AA scenes seemed to just baffle them; most of the student body at St. Irenaeus was there because of drugs and alcohol in the first place, of course. The idea of quitting or getting God to help them quit (indeed, the idea that God even *was* anybody) was way beyond their grasp. But they loved moving the simple props around and dressing and undressing in front of the audience; this, they intuitively felt, must be what went on back in NYC, in the depths of the Village that was forbidden to them because of their age. *Avant-garde!*

The only critic in attendance was a student journalist. According to him, in his review in the student newspaper, the play was a smashing success among the student body. With the faculty, not so much. Still, our student reviewer could not say enough about it: "It moved with an inevitability both ancient and modern toward a crescendo of cascading ambiguities that exquisitely dashed one's inherent nihilism."

Sylvia Cronin was put on paid administrative leave for the duration of her contract. She took advantage of this opportunity to write her first successful stage play, which opened off-Broadway, eventually moved to the Helen Hays, and subsequently earned her a Tony.

Belgium
The Cloisters of St. Mary Magdalene

The next production of the play was undertaken by an order of cloistered Benedictine nuns in Belgium. Established in 1312, the Cloisters of St. Mary Magdalene focus almost exclusively on chanting the Divine Office. People come from near and far to hear them chant in their ancient monastic church, the acoustics of which have been compared to heaven. They had previously produced two popular albums of chant; the Office for Christmas has sold more than one million copies.

It is not surprising, then, that the European cognoscenti had somehow become alerted of the production, because everyone who was anyone in contemporary music, drama, and theology on the Continent was there. Both male and female parts were played by the nuns, of course. Proper blue jeans were ordered from the United States. The official account reported that while nobody got naked, the young nun who played Eve stripped down to just the curious garments that nuns wear under their habits. Those who were actually there gave a much different account.

The Belgian nuns staged Matins at 3:00 AM, as in the old days. Then there was a long intermission, followed by the staging of Lauds at 6:51 AM precisely, to synchronize with the rising sun. This is quite a bit to ask of one's audience. Remember, however, this was a theater-going crowd. One of those privileged to be in attendance was the famed French director Antoine Lascaux, on which the play seemed to have a rather profound effect.

The Magdalenes were serious musicians, and it seems that the penny whistle and the bagpipe pieces were themselves worth the trek to the hinterland and the inconvenience of getting up at 2:30 AM to make first curtain. Their chant seemed to envelop the crude stage and lift it up to the status of a vision.

The part of the abbot fell flat, however. Apparently Belgian nuns are not accustomed to joshing around with legitimately invested authority, and therefore just didn't *get* it. They did seem to have some grasp of alcoholism, but AA, they did *not* get; it was presented like a curious ritual from a distant land. Several commentators felt that this enhanced rather than detracted from the play.

The Greek chorus was presented as a group of clueless secular nuns. It is unclear whether this was intentional or not. Do cloistered nuns consider secular nuns clueless? The nuns, of course, saw no reason to soft-pedal the death and resurrection of Christ, giving such full throat to his passion, that the story of the dying alcoholic on stage seemed like a shadow cast by the cross.

Curiously, the Belgian production also ended with rifle fire and broken glass, a most interesting interpretation. Here we had more of a feeling of Saracens at the gates, rather than a mad man on the lawn. And here also the gunfire concluded Lauds instead of preceding and aborting it, as in the original production.

After Lauds, the nuns served croissants, demi-tasse, and their own pear preserves. To have been there became the hallmark of a serious intellectual that theater season — in short, ground zero.

France

The Sorbonne

As noted prior, one of those present in Belgium was Antoine Lascaux. This was during his guest lectureship in Experimental Theater at the Sorbonne, and upon the final curtain at the Cloisters, he had already resolved to stage it himself. He produced Matins only, which he said "encompassed the essential phenomenological and dramaturgical validity" of the work. That phrase loses something in translation.

Anyway, Lascaux devoted a great deal of attention to lighting the stage, leaving the monastic choir almost completely in the dark. He really liked the Greek chorus ("it connects drama to its original roots") and added a couple of new episodes of his own which highlighted the tension between the drama of the Gospel and the saga of alcoholic drinking.

His Eve was nude alright: her nakedness veritably spilled in a puddle around the stage. He also had Adam naked, as logic would suggest, although this feature was not in the original script. This spurred several arguments of taste among those who attended both this and the prior production: Is the scene more or less erotic with Eve naked and Adam wearing a pair of jeans?

The Greek chorus seemed to emerge from Lascaux's darkened choir as if from the distant past. And by his clever lighting of the stage, his actors were etched into the darkness like ancient cave art. He had also contrived that the giant rosary framing the stage should rotate during the performance. It turned with a kind of soft mechanical clickety-clack.

In a later interview, Lascaux admitted that he himself is

an alcoholic and that he used to pray the rosary as a teenager (he thought he had a vocation). He has taken it up again since producing *Rose Fire* and has found in it "gratuitous refractions and elusive depth, like a kaleidoscope, or those scenes that jump out at you on the Olde Mill ride at the fair."

Lascaux is also notable for the food fight he got into with the papal nuncio to France over what constitutes blasphemy. A video of his production found its way onto the internet and developed quite a cult following, especially in Vietnam (which is, of course, a former French colony). During the production, the actors off stage smoked cigarettes, adding an eeriness to the darkness. Only in France.

Mississippi
St. Thaddeus

St. Thaddeus is a very small, all-black college run by the Jesuits in Mississippi. The institution dates to the days when black students had very few options for college. It survived into the modern era because of its lovely campus and legacy enrollment; more recently, segregation has begun to acquire a new cache, so student recruitment is on an upswing again. A College of Martin Luther alumnus is now the president of the college, and this may account for the fact that the drama department undertook to produce the work, in cooperation with the music department.

Taking the script as a mere starting point, St. Thaddeus improvised quite a bit. For example, they substituted gospel music for chant, singing the Psalms to the rhythms that have rocked the backwoods of Mississippi for centuries. Like the upstate New York production, they performed the Greek chorus as a rap.

The choir monks (some of whom were women, because of the relatively small size of the music department), danced and swayed to the music, and sometimes broke out of their choir stalls and rushed forward to surround the stage, still singing. All the drinking was presented in terms of the old moonshine days, and the AA scenes were Bible Belt AA with much "Amen, brother," "Praise Jesus" and similar thrown in.

By all accounts, the naked Eve was beautiful beyond belief, lighted only dimly in the pitch dark. The local ultra-conservative archdiocesan newspaper was scandalized by "the nude black virgin on stage." The archbishop blew his stack.

This aged and incensed archbishop was determined to

level the campus in revenge but abruptly died of apoplexy instead. By the time he was replaced, by a former auxiliary bishop of Cleveland, the whole thing had more or less been forgotten, the new archbishop having a number of other more pressing problems to deal with, in any case.

The thing got quite a spread in the college yearbook, without a hint of any scandal. They included a lovely black-and-white photograph of the final scene, with Eve/Mary/Em sprawled on the floor, covered in blood, and the detectives standing around in exaggerated black fedoras, examining the murdered woman's cheap plastic rosary, which had been repaired in two places, once with a paper clip, and once with dental floss.

Bibliography

Dominic of Prussia, 1382 or 1384- 1460 or 1461. *Liber experientiae /
Dominicus de Prussia.* Salzburg: Institute FÜR Anglistik und
Amerikanistik, Universität Salzberg, 2010. Series (Analecta
Cartusiana, 0253-1593: 283.)

The Hours of the Divine Office in English and Latin. Vol. 3.
Collegeville: The Liturgical Press, 1964. (pp. 1625-1641)

Palladius, Bishop of Aspuna. *Palladius: The Lausiac History.* Trans.
Robert T. Meyer. Westminster: The Newman Press, 1965. (pp.
70-71)

Pope Paul VI. *Marialis Cultus.* February 2, 1975. (paras. 38, 43 and
44)

Roberts, Karen Barbara. *The Influence of the Rosary Devotion on
Grünewald's Isenheim altarpiece.* Ph.D. Thesis. State University
of New York at Binghamton, 1985.

de Rupe, Alanus. *Unser lieben frauen Psalter [Psalterium Virginis
Mariae].* Ulm: Conrad Dinckmut, 1483.**

Winston-Allen, Anne. "Origins of the Rosary." *Month.* January,
1998. (pp. 13-17)

Winston-Allen, Anne. *Stories of the Rose: The Making of the Rosary in
the Middle Ages.* University Park: University of Pennsylvania
Press, 1997.

**Contains the original woodcuts. Note that later editions (e.g., Augsburg, Anton
Sorg, 1492; Zissenmair, 1502) have the same pictures carved by different artists;
woodcuts wear out.

About the Author

Peter Huyck is the author of *Scriptural Meditations for the Rosary* (Mystic, Connecticut: Twenty-Third Publications, 1982), *Rosary Psalms* (St. Paul's, United Kingdom, 1994), and *A Scriptural Rosary – 1596* (St. Paul's, United Kingdom, 1999). He lives in Iowa City, Iowa.

CPSIA information can be obtained
at www.ICGtesting.com
Printed in the USA
LVHW091256181019
634635LV00001B/55/P